Mindless

By
R.W.K. Clark

This is a work of fiction. All names, characters, locales, and incidents are
the product of the author's imagination and any resemblance to actual
people, places or events is coincidental or fictionalized.
Published in the United States by Clarkltd.
Po Box 45313 Rio Rancho, NM 87174
info@clarkltd.com

Edition 1
United States Copyright Office
1-6833275322 Aug 2018

Library of Congress Control Number:
2018909902
International Standard Book Numbers
ISBN-13: 978-1948312257 (Amazon)
ISBN-13: 978-1948312264 (Paperback)
ISBN-13: 978-1948312271 (Hardback)
ASIN: B07GVMW254

/200801

CONTENTS

ACKNOWLEDGMENTS

I dedicate this novel to my wonderful readers and for all the amazing people I've met and those I haven't. To my family and loved ones, all your support will not be forgotten.

This book was made possible by reviews from readers like you.

Thank you

R.W.K. Clark

PROLOGUE

"Mr. Frink, in your opinion, what was the main reason for the discontinuation of the lobotomization procedure in both medical and psychiatric practices?" Professor Stanton had his steely-eyed stare set on Melvin, his nose crinkled up. The man had that look on his face perpetually, so none of the students even took it personally; it was as though he felt that way about himself, not them.

Melvin adjusted himself in his seat and met the man's gaze. "Well, Professor Stanton, while there were several methods of lobotomy used between approximately 1890 and the middle of the 20th century, the use of them dwindled out dramatically for a number of reasons. One of the most important reasons was the introduction of psychosomatic medications which were able to induce the same effects of the neurosurgical method. But the most dominant reason came in the form of resistance on the part of medical, psychiatric, and neurology professionals who simply believed that, due to such an erratic array of outcomes, there just had to be another solution."

Stanton screwed up his nose, even more, twisted the

end of his handlebar mustache, and considered his favorite student's answer. "Not bad, Frink. But you failed to even mention the fact that, while there were seemingly successful outcomes, there were many that resulted in tragedy. However, I suppose that your statement regarding... how did you state it... "the erratic array of outcomes..." comes about as close to what I am looking for as you can get. Well done. Now, Miss Jansen, what do you feel was the best method of lobotomization used at that time?"

Melvin Frink's attention faded as soon as Professor Stanton addressed Naomi Jansen, and he sat quietly, basking in the glory of his hero's approval. Professor Stanton was one of the foremost neurologists in the country at one time. Now, in his older age, he opted to instruct psychiatric medical students at Johns Hopkins University, which was, in itself, no small feat, by any means. Receiving any kind of approval by the man was enough to send Frink flying through the ceiling and into the clouds of heaven. He was in a reverie. So caught up in it, he was, that he almost missed the fact that the class ended, and it was only the bustling of the students around him that caught his attention. A quick glance at his watch almost sent him into a panic; he was going to be late for luncheon with his mother if he didn't get a move on it, and he never missed a luncheon with Adele Frink... never.

Melvin biked from campus across town every afternoon for this purpose alone. He didn't care for the bus, as it made him feel a bit boxed in; he had a small case of social anxiety and preferred the time for thought that the bicycle ride gave him. Some of the other students in his classes teased him incessantly about the bike, but he couldn't care less. There would be plenty of times for automobiles after he was finished with school and practicing legitimately, but for now, he would stick with pedaling.

Melvin stopped at the corner of Lombard Street and Bayview Boulevard to wait for the crossing light. It was there that Jennifer Tiller came running up behind him, obviously intent on catching the bus that was due to stop there in only a few minutes.

Panting, she smiled at him. Wow, was she a looker! She had long brown hair that was typically pulled back into a bouncing ponytail, which hung down her back in great curls. Her blue eyes always seemed to shine with happiness, and her perfect teeth lit up her entire face. Melvin has had a crush on her since their very first year at Johns Hopkins, but he knew, deep inside, that he didn't stand a chance with her. His thick glasses, awkward stumbling over his own words, and odd-duck haircut didn't help, but riding a bicycle certainly wasn't impressive either, especially in a world where other men his age were driving sports cars given to them by their parents when they graduated their first four years of college. No, there was no competition as far as Melvin Frink was concerned.

"I almost didn't make it; see, there's the bus, only two blocks away. Whew!" Jennifer laughed, and it was light and lilting. It made him want to hug her right then and there. "Why don't you bus, Melvin?"

He laughed, a sound that was shy and off-beat. "I like the exercise." He left out the part that his mother thought automobiles were instruments of the devil brought on to do nothing more than steal the sons of lonely widows away in terrible accidents. While he adored Adele Frink, he could hardly wait to finally begin a private practice, somewhere away from Baltimore so he could be far, far away from her suffocating "love." Maybe he would move back to Boston, but that wouldn't do, now would it? No, the fact was that he would no more put the key in the lock of his new home for the first time then she would show up at his door in her fancy white limousine asking if he had wallpapered her new room in deep red and gold, and did the new curtains match?

No, there would be no escape until she was dead; he would live with her in her massive, cold house until then.

The bus neared the corner stop faster than he would have liked. She smelled so good, and every time the wind blew through her hair, the beautiful aroma threatened to put him into a catatonic daze. Pulling his thoughts back to the here and now, Melvin quickly turned to Jennifer just as the bus came to a complete stop.

"How about pizza?" She looked confused, and he laughed nervously. "I mean, how about we have pizza... out... sometime?"

She stared at him silently for a moment, her head

cocked as if she were trying to figure out if he were joking with her or not. After a bit, she broke her silence, and Melvin braced himself. He was used to rejection, but he wasn't always prepared for what form it would come in.

"You and me?" she asked simply, still looking at him in disbelief.

He shrugged and shifted his eyes to the bus driver, who was glaring impatiently. "Uh, yeah." He shrugged again and pushed his brown tortoiseshell glasses up his nose; he was beginning to sweat.

"I'm sorry, Melvin," she said with false regret. "I'm kind of seeing someone, and you know how…"

"…that can go," he finished. "No problem. Um, you'd better get on the bus; I think the driver is considering making you walk." He chuckled as if to show her that her refusal didn't matter to him in the slightest.

With nothing more than a half-smile, the beautiful Jennifer Tiller climbed aboard the bus, shot him a look of pity over her shoulder, and then disappeared behind the closing of the door. Embarrassed, Melvin looked around to make sure no one had witnessed the exchange, and when he was satisfied, pushed the situation from his mind and pulled his phone and earbuds from his jacket pocket. Quickly, he buried the tiny plastic wads into his ears and pulled up his playlist. Boston was his favorite band since he was originally from Boston, and they always seemed to have something to say about situations like this. He started it from the beginning. It was the entire "Boston" album which would play first, their original, starting out with "More Than A Feeling." Well, maybe that wasn't the most appropriate tune at the moment.

He lived with his mother in an old seven-bedroom mansion on Greenway, in Guilford. It was only a twelve-minute drive home from Johns Hopkins, but of course, he didn't drive. Fortunately, he could ride his bike through the park and save a few minutes. Melvin Frink was proud of the fact that he could make the trek home, with the shortcut, in under six minutes.

If he didn't stop to talk to snobbish females, of course.

As he neared the corner where he would cross to get to the park, he saw the blockades in the street. What the heck was going on? From where he was, it looked as though he wouldn't be cutting through the park at all! Mother would be upset. He dug out his cell to call her and let her know he was running a bit late. As he swiped the screen on, he noticed that there was a line of pedestrians being guided across in the direction of Guilford Gateway Park, making their way across St. Paul Street. He brought his bike to a stop and watched as the line finished, and a man acting like some distorted version of a crossing guard, reversed the direction the pedestrians were going; he now led a line consisting of a mother and four kids across. He decided to wait and cross St. Paul on the next round. Locking his phone because he knew he wouldn't be as late as he anticipated, he shoved it into his jacket and pulled his left earbud from his ear.

That was when Melvin Frink heard a sound that was akin to an explosion, and it came from right above his head, deafening and stunning him at the same time. His head snapped back to make sense of the sound; he was oblivious to the chaos and workmen running toward him. Instead, he just looked up.

The beam, which had been supported twenty feet over his head with heavy cables only moments before, struck him in the forehead before he could even register what it was. Just as it came into contact with him, a workman jumped under it, as if he were trying to slide into home base. He knocked Melvin backward, who was already unconscious, thankfully. He didn't even feel the wind leave his body when he hit the ground, and he didn't feel the weight of the beam as it not only severed the workman into two pieces but crushed both of Melvin's feet.

Melvin didn't hear the screaming or crying, didn't have a clue when the emergency units showed up and had no recollection of police tearing through his wallet and briefcase to determine who was this unconscious person, gushing blood from his head, and lying with mangled feet beneath the heavy torso of a dead thirty-five-year-old construction foreman.

As a matter of fact, Melvin Dennis Frink wasn't aware of anything after then for a very, very long time.

CHAPTER 1

It was so disorienting... the smells, the distant voices. He had the overwhelming desire to get up and pee, but eventually, that would leave him (who knows how), and he would leave his own consciousness behind him. Sometimes, the voices came from people who seemed to mill around him incessantly, debating whether he would ever wake, or if his mother would have to opt to "pull the plug." It had to be one of the worst nightmares he had ever had in his life, and it seemed to last forever.

Melvin had tubes in his nose, one in his throat, and one in his stomach. He was keenly aware, even in his state, that there was a constant and consistent beeping going on, right next to him, at all times. He was convinced... it took nothing more than this to pull an individual into the belief that they had died and gone straight to hell. The real hell, not the hell in comic books and biblical descriptions. But a place where you are helpless, burning, you can't communicate, and you always seem to have to pee.

It also seemed that his eyes were constantly closed, keeping him in a state of darkness that he couldn't explain. He couldn't turn his head, couldn't move his lips, couldn't even blink. Maybe he was dead; at least, that was one of the most logical explanations he could come up with. But with the intercoms that kept calling for doctors and code blues and everything else, he came to realize that death was not at all what he was experiencing.

At first, he could recall nothing, including his name, and his mind scrambled incessantly until that finally came to him. It happened on a day when he heard the voice of his mother speaking to a man and woman; their voices were directly above him.

"Doctor, I really don't care how long we have to keep him like this," her snooty voice was saying, as though she were speaking from the end of a long tunnel. "Money is no object, and I will not have my son put down, as it is called, just because you want to rotate your beloved beds."

Yes, it was his mother's voice, alright. What was her name? If only he could recall it, surely his own name would come back to him. After all, he knew the voice to be his mother's: the nasally, holier-than-thou tone, the demanding attitude that always made others around her feel as though they just weren't good enough to even be in her presence. Yes, it was definitely her.

The "doctor" she was speaking to replied, "Mrs. Frink, it's not that we don't want to care for your son, and it really isn't about the money —"

She suddenly cut him off. "Poppycock, doctor. Of course, it is."

Frink! That was his last name: Frink! Of course, he was… he was…

"My dear Melvin is worth every penny in the world to me, and much, much more. I would think that a substantial donation would motivate you to see things my way, don't you?"

Yes, his name was Melvin Frink; his middle name didn't even matter, nor did the question of it enter his mind in any way. Melvin Frink. Even though he couldn't move his lips or say it aloud, it felt right in his soul, and he was overjoyed. Now, if only he could sit up and join these imbeciles in the conversation, they were having about him. Obviously, this physician thought he was absent from the body. Was he plugged into the wall or something? He didn't care, but he would rather die than be released in any way, shape, or form to his mother.

"Madam, I am simply suggesting that in Melvin's current state the best thing that can be done is to make him as comfortable as possible. Here, at Meadows Community Hospital, we can provide him with much of that comfort, but we are not a long-term care facility, Mrs. Frink, and Melvin has already been here for three years!"

Suddenly, it was as though Melvin's heart stopped beating in his chest. Three years? Three years at Meadows Community? What had happened? Why was he here? He began to feel a fit of anger rise up in his chest that he had never experienced before, and there was nothing, absolutely nothing he could do to express it, nothing he could say on his own behalf.

"Well, Doctor." Adele Frink sniffed loudly with disdain. "Now, I will give you credit for keeping him with us, and you have done a sufficient job as far as his personal care during this long period. But I certainly cannot take full responsibility for him... alone... at our home. I mean, don't get me wrong, but..."

"Mrs. Frink, I was suggesting a nice long-term care facility that is equipped for patients such as Melvin, with a professional staff who would treat him like a member of their own family. Since money, as you say, is no object —"

"Oh, hush, if you please, Dr. Fitzsimmons! Your condescension and sass do not evade my intellect or my grasp." Adele was pretty much spitting fire, and the "unconscious" Melvin could almost see the vile look on her face as she spoke to the man.

The doctor, his mother, and anyone else who may have been in the room fell silent, but Melvin could hear his mother's sensible heels clicking back and forth as she paced the institutionally tiled floor. At last, she stopped next to the bed once again.

"I dread to think that this young lady, and how many others, have had to clean his messes, bathe him, dress him... how many of them have seen him naked? He would be so terribly embarrassed." Adele paused again before continuing; now she was beginning to turn on the fake, manipulative tears and added a slight whine to her voice. "Now you want my son to be exposed to this with an entirely new set of people. Did you know that he was studying, with honors, to be a psychosurgeon?"

"Ma'am, psychosurgery is really no longer –"

"Quiet!" she spat. "You know what, Doctor Fitzsimmons? Forget any potential endowments or donations, and I loathe every harlot nurse you have working under this roof. You disgust me, all of you. Have my son ready to be transferred home by tomorrow evening, and I will see to it that he has the best live-in care possible. And you can bet your substandard derrière that it won't be some overeducated Scarlet-woman like the one who stands here with us now. Tell me, dear, how many times have you sat on top of my son and had your way? Hmmm?"

All Melvin could hear was the whimpering of a younger woman, and the padded steps of her soft-soled shoes as the girl ran from the room. He wanted to reach up and punch his mother's dental implants right from her gums.

"Mrs. Frink, it will be my pleasure to do just that," Dr. Fitzsimmons replied, stifling his own anger. "In the meantime, I expect that you will limit all contact with the staff of this hospital to that which is only extremely necessary. When would you like him ready for transfer?"

"By seven-thirty tomorrow evening," she hissed. "The bill will be settled before he leaves the building… good day."

The doctor left, and a helpless, seemingly comatose Melvin lay helpless as his mother began to rapidly kiss his cheeks and forehead. He could smell cigarettes on her breath, and a bit of gin, too. He also knew she was leaving fuchsia lipstick prints all over his face, and it made him want to vomit, but even that was no use. Now he had to go home with her! He would rather die in a nursing home...

Melvin Dennis Frink spent the rest of that night, and, until shortly after his tube-fed breakfast, the following day wallowing in self-pity, anger, and frustration. The truth was, aside from a bit of impatience with his mother now and then throughout his life, he really had never known anger. He wouldn't call this anger, though; he was furious. His entire life was out of his hands.

At least, it was... until eight in the morning on the day he was to go home to the horrible Adele.

CHAPTER 2

His tube feeding had just ended, and the nurse, whom he couldn't see, was cleaning him up from the meal if you could call pureed pancakes and custard a breakfast. She hummed to herself as she worked, then, when his face was presentable, she set about preparing the equipment for his sponge bath. All the time, she continued to hum. It was a tune he thought he knew, and it was one he was sure he hated in his past life if indeed he had one. It was some Simon and Garfunkel song about a camera or something.

Melvin groaned in displeasure.

Immediately, the nurse stopped the humming, and the sponge with which she had been gently scrubbing his right armpit stopped dead in its tracks. He could feel the warm water trickling down his ribs and beneath his shoulder, and this annoyed him even more. Melvin tried to jerk away slightly, but he was weak… so very weak.

"M-M-Mr. Frink?" The woman sounded scared to death. "Mr. Frink, can you hear me?" With even more frustration than before, he groaned loudly. His voice was no more than a gravelly whisper, his face twisted into a grimace of pain at the very sound of her voice.

He could hear her breathing rapidly. "Mr. Frink, I'm nurse Shelly Mason." He heard a splashing sound as she dropped the sponge into the bowl of warm water on the bedside table. "Mr. Frink, can you hear me?"

His eyeballs moved around beneath the lids; he wanted so badly to open them and look at her and tell her "Yes, I can hear you! The entire place can hear you!" But he couldn't even muster the strength to open them. Next, he began to try to move his lips around, and he was suddenly keenly aware of the tube buried down his throat. He growled as best he could and began to move the fingers on his right hand slightly as if trying to shoo her away.

Shelly Mason quickly took him by the wrist and checked his pulse; it was thready but unmistakably strong. Next, she gave all of his life support equipment a once-over, and from what she could see, she was witnessing a miracle. Was this man breathing on his own? How could that be? Bending over, she put her ear close to his tube-filled nose, and she could tell he was actively taking in oxygen.

Suddenly, she was scrambling for the call button. She must have pushed it because all Melvin could hear was her voice, almost hysterical, calling for help. Next, she dropped the useless device, and he heard her feet pitter-patter fast to the door of his room.

"I need a doctor!" she shouted. "Is Dr. Fitzsimmons on the unit yet? Are there any available physicians? We have one rising in here!"

It seemed to Melvin that all hell broke loose right

then. Suddenly, the room was filled with people, and though he couldn't see them, he could hear the jumbled confusion of their voices as they tried to verify what the nurse was telling them. He was being poked, prodded, and asked questions which he was directed to answer with hand squeezes. The voices were filled with elated excitement: yes, yes, this long-time accident victim, this man with such a severe head injury that they never thought he would see the light of day again, was beginning to come to. Sure, no one had any idea how he would be when he fully woke, but any setbacks could be dealt with, they were saying.

This went on for two hours: testing, talking, hand squeezing, and more testing. They took blood from him, subjected him to x-rays and MRIs, then tube fed him some more. The only one that seemed to be missing from the group, much to his relief, was his bossy, over-bearing mother, and he couldn't help but thank whatever power was suspended over the universe that he hadn't woken up while in her home or presence. He would have likely committed suicide right then.

Unfortunately, she was there before he knew it. Dr. Fitzsimmons and his team spoke with her out in the hall, but the door was slightly ajar so Melvin could hear the gist of the conversation. They were telling her he needed time; he would need therapy on all of life's levels before he would be able to return home. Taking him from Meadows Community right then would be detrimental to his recovery. Of course, Adele Frink nagged and bitched, but when Dr. Fitzsimmons went so far as to threaten to get a court order to stop her from taking him, the old broad shut right up, and after a short time, he allowed the woman to see her son, but only with him present.

Melvin heard a chair pulling up next to the bed, and he turned his head slightly in its direction.

"Melvin, dear, it's Mummy," she began. She reached up and took him by the hand gently, then continued. "It seems you are coming back to us now. I'm so sorry, love, but you will have to remain here for a bit longer. But as your mother, I must ask, do you want to come home? I can hire any therapist you may need."

Dr. Fitzsimmons interjected. "Melvin, give her two light squeezes for yes, and a single one for no. The choice is yours, son."

Adele continued to hold his hand, but said to the physician, "Are you sure he even knows what you're saying? For all we know, these are random muscle spasms!"

"We've been communicating with him all day," he replied softly, yet firmly. "He will answer you."

Adele paused. "Well, Melvin, do you want Mummy to take you home?"

All at once, he gave her hand a single squeeze. He squeezed her so hard that her hands were nearly crushed, and Adele Frink cried out in pain. She tried to extract herself from his grasp, her eyes glued to his face, but he would not let go. He just squeezed harder and harder.

As she stared at him, crying in pain, he began to

smile.

Dr. Fitzsimmons was there immediately, his soothing voice distracting Melvin from the rage he felt toward the ever-controlling woman seated next to him. Gently, he pried her hand from Melvin's, and the woman whimpered, tears falling down her face. Melvin's smile remained, but his hand went limp.

Fitzsimmons escorted Adele out to the hall. "It's going to take time; brain injury survivors most always suffer a severe change in personality. Why don't you go get a coffee from the waiting room? I'll be in to look at your hand in no time."

With that, the woman wandered off in a daze, rubbing her bruised and swollen hand. Fitzsimmons ordered one of the nurses to make sure he was comfortable. He also warned the woman to be careful; Melvin seemed a bit aggressive.

As the nurse carried out his orders, Fitzsimmons watched through the door. The patient had acted with severe aggression, and he had seemed pleased to do it. But it was too soon to tell; it would take time. But nothing about the behavior Melvin had demonstrated was reflective of the young man his mother or college acquaintances had described before his brain surgery.

∞

"There, there, my dear. Is your bed comfortable enough? I made sure that Nurse Conroy fluffed the pillows just the way you have always liked them." Adele Frink fussed and hovered over Melvin as he lay in a brand new adjustable bed in the room he had lived in for most of his life, staring at the ceiling, not sure how to feel. "Are they fluffed enough for you, Melvin, dear?"

Melvin didn't move a muscle, except for slightly twitching his lip. With his eyes still fastened on the ceiling, he replied, "I feel like I'm going to sink down into the damn things and suffocate; they're so soft."

Adele flinched at his use of vulgarity. Her Melvin had never spoken this way, the doctors warned her that the surgery would change his personality some, when and if he ever came out of the coma. Well, he had come out of it, and being vulgar was just one of the changes she had noticed. Mainly, he seemed like a different person all around. He was angry, hateful, and at times, even volatile, throwing his eating utensils or plate of food, or whatever was closest to him when he came unglued.

Melvin had ended up staying in the hospital a mere four weeks for therapy before Adele demanded that she finally take him home. He hadn't wanted to come, but here he was, and he wasn't happy about it. Instead of being relieved or happy, Melvin showed hostility and resentment. When she tried to talk to him about why this was, all he would say was that anyone who had to tolerate her coddling and obsessing would act the same way. She had excused herself from him when he said that and made her way to the restroom, where she cried for ten minutes.

During his month at Meadows Community Hospital after waking, his biggest focus was working on physical therapy and improving his cognitive and mental skills.

Melvin noticed that the doctors seemed particularly interested in his brain function, and he attributed this to the fact that he had suffered a fairly severe brain injury. During his second week, he began to read (as much as he was able) about his condition, and it was simple to pinpoint certain things that were obvious symptom-wise. But certain things didn't make sense to him at all, and because of his condition, it was difficult for him to make heads or tails of those things and sort them out. He would give it time, then take his questions and concerns to his doctor at a later time, he figured.

There was one thing that was prevalent, though, and while it disturbed him greatly, it also brought him strange feelings of peace and gratification. It was this overwhelming desire to cause pain, the pain of any kind. From something as simple as shooting his mother a glare of hatred and making her run from him in tears to the squeezing of her hand at the hospital until it was bruised and swollen. As a matter of fact, most of his days (and nights) consisted of daydreaming of hurting anyone and everyone he could think of. But with each passing day of drudgery in his mother's house, these fantasies grew into horrid wide-awake nightmares that brought smiles of pleasure to his face. If the doctors and therapists, Nurse Conroy, or even his own mother were aware of some of the hellish mental visions he entertained, they would likely have him locked up for the rest of his life. But he didn't have to worry about that right now… he just needed to keep his little daydreams to himself.

But they came on quickly and randomly, with no provocation of any kind. One example was when his mother spoke to him about the stupid fluffing of the pillows. The reason he was so irritated by it wasn't that he couldn't care less about the pillows, or that they were too flat or stiff; he was annoyed to his very core by the fact that she was interrupting one of those very pleasant mini-movies in his brain, this one about his mother herself. He had been envisioning tearing her toenails out, one by one, and pausing between each to wallow in her screams. Her interruption, and his need to make her go away caused the fantasy to grow. By the time she left the room, he was able to refocus his thoughts, he began to picture himself tying her down, wide awake, and slicing her stomach open so he could play with her inners. Yes, that would be good. He would keep her alive, in a box, plugged into the wall as she had done to him, and play with her intestines whenever the urge came over him. He had giggled out loud at the thought, which caused Nurse Conroy to give him a nervous look and skitter from the room as fast as her white shoe-covered feet would carry her body.

The constant anger and irritation he felt were almost physical in nature, as though someone was rubbing sandpaper over his flesh. This was something that had been with him since he woke, and he couldn't figure it out. Slowly, but surely, bits and pieces of memory of his former life came back to him, and it seemed that, aside from his mother getting on his nerves, Melvin had really never gotten angry about much. He remembered being such an easy going guy that even outright insults didn't bother him much, and he got them often, due to his odd personality. What had caused this drastic emotional change? Sure, from what he'd read and learned, it could have been the brain injury, but to this extreme? No, he was educated enough from his time in college and medical school, then at Johns Hopkins, to know that this constant abrasion on his soul from the inside out had to be more than that. The truth was, he had no idea what lengths his mother had gone to, underhandedly and selfishly, to keep him with her. If he had, everything would have made perfect sense.

But for now, Melvin was doing well, for all intents and purposes. Therapy had him walking again, jerkily, granted, and he tired quickly, but he was walking. He was also gaining strength back in his limbs every day, and even though he spoke with a slight stutter, his thoughts seemed much clearer than they were the day he first regained consciousness. Would he ever be anything like the Melvin he was before? He wondered this often. But only time would tell.

R.W.K. Clark

CHAPTER 3

Melvin grunted slightly as he pushed himself up off the edge of the king-sized bed. Nurse Conroy (or Doris, as she insisted he call her when his mother wasn't around) had opened the draperies when she brought him his breakfast. At first, the soft light had been pleasant, but now the sun was beating through the panes, and it made his head feel as though a thousand knives were stabbing into his brain. Squinting hard, he stood, a bit shaky at first, then slowly began to shuffle over to close them when he felt stable enough on his feet. The mornings were always the hardest for him when it came to physical strength. By nine or nine-thirty, however, his slight limp was barely noticeable, and the shuffle in his step would completely disappear.

As it turned out, Doris Conroy had grown on Melvin quite nicely. Though he frequently caught her looking at him with paranoia out of the corner of her eye, he didn't blame her. After all, as a nurse, she was familiar with the lifelong after-effects of traumatic brain injury; victims' moods swung at the drop of a hat, and the outcomes had been known to be scary and violent, sometimes deadly. While he still got flashes of violent thoughts regarding the woman, they had become fewer and farther between. She was a woman of about fifty, as he learned, soft-hearted, and had six grandchildren whom she adored. When his mother was outspending his deceased father's fortune, which occurred in one manner or another on a daily basis, Melvin and Nurse Conroy would chat a bit. Just superficial topics in the beginning, but by the time a couple of months had passed, it seemed they had become old friends. If Melvin were honest, he would have to admit that he wished she had been his mother. Her children lived out on their own, with families and personal responsibilities and dreams that she supported fully. Adele Frink would rather hold Melvin hostage to his death; only then, he believed wholly, would she be satisfied. She had even nagged him to death about his medical studies, begging him to quit and spend his days with her full-time. Continuing on to become a surgeon had been the only thing Melvin had insisted upon in his life, and it came at a torturously nagging price daily. Now, though, Adele couldn't be happier; he was snugly under her thumb, squirming for his life, and she would keep it that way for as long as she possibly could.

Melvin drew the drapes closed and chuckled about his own thoughts. He hated his mother. What he felt toward her fit the definition given by Webster, so hate was the word he used in his thoughts. But he also loved her; after all, she was his mother, and he knew she cherished him. Adele Frink simply showed it in a very unhealthy manner, and from what he understood, she was only behaving toward him in the same manner her father had behaved toward her when her own mother had died. She believed she was parenting him properly, even though her every motivation was selfish as far as he was concerned. He wanted her dead, but he never wanted her to be gone. It was a strange mix of emotions indeed.

With the drapes closed, he crossed the room and turned on the overhead chandelier. Right then, Nurse Conroy came into the room, after a brief knock on his door and a call of his name. She poked her head through the door and smiled at him.

"I'm sorry, Melvin, dear," she said. "I didn't mean to just walk in like this; you're still in your pajamas. I just wanted to be sure that you had eaten. You know what your mother would say if she came home and you hadn't."

He smiled back at her and shoved a random thought of slamming her head in the door out of his mind. "No, Doris; you're never a problem. I had to close the drapes… the sun." Melvin turned and fetched the tray with his empty breakfast plates and glasses for her, then carried it over to where she stood. "Here you go; Mother should give us both an "all clear" for now. Who's to say what will happen later?"

Doris winked at him, enjoying the little jokes about Adele's suffocative ways. "Fine, dear. I'll just get this out of the way and let you lie back down if you wish. Oh, good! You took your medication! I just hate fighting with your mother when you don't."

"I know she blames you," he replied sympathetically. "Don't worry... I'll take it if only to keep her off your back. You know, I'm going to dress and get out of the room today. How long is Mother supposed to be gone?"

Doris knit her brow in thought. "Let's see, she was going to do some browsing at the Lexington Market before her luncheon appointment with Dr. Arondale. Oh, yes, she also said she may spend some time at Towson Town Center Mall if she couldn't find anything good at Lexington. I don't expect her back until nearly two if she stays true to form."

"Another appointment with Philip Arondale? She must be having anxiety about me again?"

Doris clucked and shook her head. "She will do that for as long as she draws breath... it's the curse of motherhood, though she may take it a bit far, it's out of love. No, she is due for her monthly prescriptions. Besides, you know how she loves to talk that poor psychiatrist's ear off, and I think he loves listening to her rantings."

"He loves her money, Doris," Melvin stated flatly. "At any rate, since she will be absent for so long, I feel like walking in the house today. I've been cooped up on this wing for so long that I am beginning to doubt there is a world out there anymore. Besides, my memories of the place are so scant... I would love to just wander and refresh the thoughts I once had. Did you know this place used to be both a mortuary and a morgue when it was built? I was fifteen when my dad passed away, and we moved here. The history of the place used to give me the good willies and fill my imagination with all kinds of fun."

Doris shuddered. "Oh, you youngsters. Now you've planted ideas in my mind that will have me seeing ghosts around every corner."

"I'll protect you," Melvin teased. "My favorite place was the basement; that was where all the work was done. There was even a special entry that allowed the hearses and medical examiners to drive right down into it. To be honest, I can barely remember what it looks like down there, but today I intend to take another look."

She shuddered again and laughed. "I have never ventured down, and now I never will. You have fun, but do one favor for me, please?"

"Of course, Doris. Anything for you."

With a motherly tone, the nurse answered, "Take your cane. If your mother came home early for any reason and thought I had let you wander without it, I would likely lose my job. Heck, she's liable to fire me just for letting you out of your room."

Melvin approached her and put a gentle hand on her cheek. A flash of thought came to him consisting of grabbing the flesh and ripping it from her face. His smile faltered, and he violently pushed it out of his mind. Immediately, fear shadowed her face, as if she had seen inside his mind. He quickly regained his composure.

"If my mother ever tries to fire you, Doris, she will

pay dearly for it." He leaned forward and gave her a peck on the cheek. "No worries, my dear. I wouldn't be able to function without you."

The look of fright and apprehension disappeared from her countenance. With a smile, she backed out of the doorway with the tray and Melvin closed the door quietly behind her. He took a deep breath and smiled broadly; the Beast was gone! Well, for several hours, anyway. He had been waiting for the time to be right and to feel strong enough to go exploring around the old place. He hadn't felt this excited in longer than he could remember, and it seemed he couldn't make it to the wardrobe fast enough to dress.

Melvin wondered if his mother had ventured into the basement for any reason since his accident. He doubted it; it was a very creepy place. It was massive, as big as the main house itself, if not bigger. There was a large steel door that opened up to a large main area, which Melvin assumed had been an office area at the time. Across the room was another door, made of wood, which was in surprisingly good shape for its age. It opened up to a long, broad corridor, all concrete. Along each side of the corridor were individual rooms, six on each side. The rooms were small, about ten feet long by seven feet wide. All of them, as far as Melvin knew, still sat just as they were left over eighty years ago, with steel exam tables in place, raised metal trays with sharp instruments lined up in order, and other necessary appliances used in the autopsy and embalming processes. Melvin specifically remembered that all of those things had been covered in a thick layer of dust, and cobwebs filled nearly every corner and crevice… he had loved it!

At the very end of the long corridor, there were three doors, at least, as far as he could remember, but his memory could be faulty. If he was correct, the only door he could remember the purpose of was the one in the center… it was unlike any other door down there. It was heavy iron and did not go all the way to the floor; it began about three feet up off the floor and was about five feet wide. Fancy, scrolled letters were molded onto the iron, but he couldn't remember what it said; he knew it was the maker of the entire contraption which the door was part of the crematory. While he had, indeed, been inside two doors that flanked the actual "oven," as he was fond of calling it, he couldn't remember what they housed… probably offices, but it would have been so hot in those rooms. He would check them out today and bring it back to his mind.

It took Melvin much longer than he anticipated getting dressed. Typically, his mother hovered over him while he attempted to clothe himself, cooing and forcing her help on him; it was humiliating, and it made him angry, but it cut the process time in half. Now she wasn't there to make him let her help, and while it took much longer, it felt freeing and invigorating. He was able to do it himself, and the amount of time it took really didn't matter. From now on, he was determined to make her let him be and give him some privacy, as it should be.

After forty minutes, Melvin found himself before the large oval full-length mirror that sat in the corner of his room, reeking of both age and old money. He combed his hair carefully and gave a second look at the clothing he had chosen to wear while prowling around the old mansion: blue jeans with a couple of wear marks at the faded knees, a plain black t-shirt, and a plaid flannel button-down, open, with the long sleeves, rolled halfway up his forearms. With his black framed glasses sitting neatly and evenly on his face, he felt ready to face his day. The only thing missing was the heavy-duty, cop-like flashlight that Doris Conroy kept on the stand just inside his bedroom door so she could check him during the night without disturbing him. Heading for the door, he grabbed the flashlight and made his way out and down the long, ornate, and heavily furnished corridor that led to the staircase leading to the second floor. His mother would prefer he take the lift, of course, but what she didn't know wouldn't hurt her. Actually, the truth was, she would be furious; she just didn't think he was able to do a damn thing on his own, which was exactly the reason he was so determined to defy her. She was so controlling.

As he stepped the final step onto the first-floor landing, Doris came around the corner with some linens in her hand. She looked at him, surprised. Melvin simply smiled sheepishly and gave her a wave with his free hand.

"Oh, aren't we the daring one today, Mr. Frink," Doris said. He could see the sparkle in her eye, but it was mingled with fear and worry. "Your mother will die if you avoid the lift, you know."

He shrugged, "I'm fine, Doris… I am taking it very slowly. I just want to look at the rest of the house on my way down. It's been so long."

"Just please don't get caught," she muttered, her eyes shifting around. "It will be my hide."

The nurse quickly disappeared back around the corner, afraid to even be in his presence for fear his mother would return. He pushed it out of his mind and began a walk around the first floor. He really had no interest in anything there; he just wanted to see how much had changed. To his surprise, everything looked exactly the same. Nothing had been moved as far as he could tell, and everything was spotless. It was still the same cold hard museum he remembered it to be.

Melvin didn't spend more than a few seconds in any one room. He peeked into the spotless kitchen with disinterest then passed through the dining room with the table that sat twenty; it was never used and looked as if that was still true. Next, he looked in the library and in his mother's study… all the same dreary perfection.

Then he rounded the final corner, and there it was: a steep set of carpeted steps which led down to a tiny landing; at the bottom was the massive basement door. An excited chill coursed down the length of his body. Standing at the top of the stairs for several minutes, he let his mind wander to his memories of the basement, which were few. As he stood there, he knew there was more to this "exploration" than he had let on to Doris… he had some plans for the basement, though he hadn't really even begun to perfect them yet. They were sort of in… daydream mode… if you will. He wanted to see if it was as he remembered because if it were, it would be perfect for him.

As he slowly and jerkily started down the narrow steps, clinging to the banister with his free hand, he wondered briefly if the door would be locked. Of course not; his mother never went anywhere near the door and even avoided the stairwell area like the plague. Besides, spooky history or not, she had never been too superstitious; she just had no purpose for that area of the house.

He counted the steps as he went, and at number seven, he thought he was going to go head over heels to the bottom. Stopping and closing his eyes, Melvin regained his bearings. He wasn't afraid of falling; it might be a blessing. No, he just didn't want his mother firing Doris Conroy because he couldn't keep his balance or sneak around properly. In seconds, he had his wits about him and continued on. Reaching the bottom, he smiled… there were thirteen steps. For some reason, he was unable to recall that fact, though he knew he must have counted the steps before. It didn't matter though; it couldn't be more perfect.

The heavy door opened easily, with only a slight creak. He made sure to close it behind him quietly, then took a deep whiff of the air around him. It was musty and spooky smelling, wonderfully macabre, especially in the dark. Reaching to the left in the darkness, he flipped a light switch that, for some reason, he knew was there, and the bulbs, ancient but working, flickered to life. The main room was dark, dismal, and dusty. It smelled slightly of mildew and faded formaldehyde, though he thought the former was in his imagination. It was morbid, and it had a bad feel to it, the place did.

Yes, it was beautiful.

So, the exploration began, and with each step, with each entry into each new room down the corridor, he knew it was fate. This was precisely what he needed to take back control of his life. The question wasn't if he would do it… the question was when.

∞

Adele Frink snapped her compact closed with a disgusted sniff and shot her eyes around the room for the twentieth time. It wasn't her reflection she was irritated with; of course, not… she looked stunning. It was the fact that Philip was late, and she hated to be kept waiting. Granted, it wasn't like Dr. Philip Arondale to be late, but to not even call and let her know that he was going to be… well, unacceptable. Once again, glancing down at her phone… nothing. She should be worried, but she felt more inconvenienced than anything, and by Philip, to top it all off!

The fact of the matter, which no one in her life was aware of, was that she and Philip Arondale had been having an ongoing affair since shortly after her husband died. At first, it was something to take her mind off the pain and fear of what happened if the money ran out.

But then it became an emotional dependency of sorts, especially after Melvin's accident. Now he was simply her glorified drug dealer. Lately, she had been asking for pills more than usual, and Philip was becoming a bit resistant. But she paid him well, the sex was fair, and the luncheons were outstanding, especially when she paid. But right now, he was doing nothing more than pissing her off.

As if on cue, her cell chirped, making her jump and look around the room self-consciously; no one was paying any attention to her. Adele picked up the device and glared at the screen... Philip, of course. How dare he!

"Where are you?" she hissed into the phone.

Philip paused on the line before clearing his throat. He spoke in a low tone, as though there were others in the room, and he didn't want his conversation to be heard.

"I'm sorry, Adele," he said in barely above a whisper. "I had a patient who attempted suicide an hour ago, and they nearly got the job done. I have been here at the Meadows in the psychiatric unit since they arrived by ambulance. I'm simply not going to make lunch."

With a loud, long sigh of disgust, she closed her eyes and sat back against the chair. "Nice. You could have called sooner. Listen, do what you have to do, but I need my pills. Have you managed to think about that at all?"

She could imagine Philip rolling his eyes in frustration; she always managed to have that effect on him. He knew he was being used, but he didn't care, as long as the checks, and the sex, kept coming. Besides, his feelings didn't matter to her at all; he was a hired hand, no more, no less.

"Like I said, I'm at the Meadows, but I'll call Julia and have her print them out and stamp my signature. Look, Adele, I really must go." He paused, as if he was considering just hanging up, then continued. "We could make up lunch tomorrow."

"Don't bother," she snapped. "I'll pick up the prescriptions in twenty minutes. Make sure the retard has them ready."

She slid her perfectly manicured finger over the screen of her smartphone and motioned for the waiter to bring her one more martini and the bill. With her nose in the air, she took the drink from the young man and slammed it while sliding her credit card across the table to him. This would certainly come out of Philip's fee, he could count on that. Now what to do with her time?

Draining her drink, she stood, grabbed her bag from the table, and left the restaurant. Philip's office was only six miles away; she would pick up her prescriptions, have them filled, and simply go home. Maybe a few pills would put her out of her misery for a while... wouldn't that be wonderful?

As she waited for the valet to bring her car, her mind went to Melvin. Hopefully, he was fed and sleeping soundly, so he wouldn't take notice when she put herself into a drug-induced coma. She would hate for him to ever see any of her weaknesses. As far as he was concerned, she could do no wrong.

CHAPTER 4

Melvin had lost track of time.

How long he had actually been in the cellar, he had no idea. All he knew was that by the time he came back to his senses from his reverie of fantasy, he had a clear picture in his head of what he was going to do with the basement. Oh, yes, he had big plans, and it was the perfect place for them.

He also had the opportunity to go through the two rooms that flanked the crematory and had been extremely pleased to find that they were filled with old supplies that had been used in autopsies, embalming, and the preparation of bodies for viewing. There were also other things, items that most of the world didn't consider would be needed during the processes following death, but they would be of great help in the journey he was about to undertake. Now, it was simply time for planning.

His stomach rumbled hard, and that was what finally snapped him out of it. He was in the second storage room at the time; digging through boxes, when an odd, excited smile came on his face. He had stuffed a couple of small bottles into his breast pocket and stood up; he wondered what Doris had made for lunch. Whatever it was, he was sure it would be delicious. He planned to take his meal in the kitchen nook; maybe he could even convince her to eat with him. Mother was gone, so the two literally had all the freedom in the world. A glance at his watch told him it was nearly one in the afternoon. Wow, he had been down there for hours! How time flies when you're having fun. He patted his pocket to make sure the bottles were there, then backed out of the storage room and closed the door softly behind him, caressing the knob as if it were a lover.

It took Melvin a long while to actually leave the basement. He stopped at each of the empty rooms and admired them, not seeing the stark spookiness of the remains left behind by the past, but envisioning what they would look like in the near future… soon, very soon.

At last, he made his way out of the heavy door and made sure it was securely closed behind him. He would have to secure it better than it was when he finally set things into motion. It wouldn't do to have anyone down there for any reason; it was his space now, and it would stay that way. After all, in a month or so, he would have free-reign of the place; not even Doris would have to be there anymore. He would make sure she received a generous severance, the kind that ensured she wouldn't have to work for the rest of her life.

A stabbing pain then hit him suddenly, just as he was turning around to start up the cellar stairs. It stung him deep in the front of his brain, in his forehead over his left eye. The eye twitched violently, tearing up to the point that tears seemed to roll out immediately. Melvin's hand shot up to his forehead as he winced and staggered back a step. He caught his footing and froze, his mind totally encompassed with the pain; his right hand was gripping the oak handrail in a blind attempt to keep himself from falling. Then the pain dulled, and slowly dwindled to a nagging itch, which caused his left eye to pulse and twitch violently before suddenly clearing, disappearing entirely. Melvin paused for a long moment, waiting for it to come again, his mind whirling with confusion. Taking a breath, he relaxed a bit and shook his head back and forth several times. It had nearly knocked him out, but now nothing more than a deep, fading itch remained. Bending down, he picked up his nearly-forgotten cane and began the journey on the steps, glancing back at the big door behind him; that was all it took to put the pain out of his mind entirely.

He had to get started... there was so much to do. It would be a feat of patience, having to sneak around his mother to accomplish it all. It would be so much easier to begin and complete if he didn't have to tap dance around her. He wanted to have it going as soon as possible because he wouldn't be able to find what he was looking for until he had the first room completed. Yes, he would only need to renovate a single room, and only slightly, before he would be able to finally find someone to... be with. He had been thinking about it for some time, dwelling on it, actually. He was lonely, very lonely, but he was keenly aware that Mother would never let him have the kind of fun that filled his mind for hours. The basement would bring his thoughts to full fruition...

Coming down the stairs had seemed to take much longer than the trip he was making back up. There was a bit of pep in his step, and the pain in his head was completely gone. He continued to ascend the steps one at a time and let himself think about what he would do. He would go looking, you see. After all, one should never just choose the first one he sees. If one wanted a pet, one needed to really look for just the right one and study it. After all, a pet should be suited to its owner in more ways than one, but he guessed that training could rectify any upset an unadjusted pet might cause. It would learn to behave and play properly, just like a good pet should. It would take away his boredom and loneliness, and entertain him in his long hours of stagnation, and much more.

It was the actual obtaining of this pet that gave him discomfort in considering, but that was only the jitters. He had never gone out and done anything like he was considering. But these jitters were greatly overpowered by the tickle he felt in his groin when he thought about it, and that was the reason it must be done. It was time for him to have what he wanted to have in his life, and right now, this was it. He could work his way around his intolerable, overbearing mother one way or another.

Reaching the top of the staircase, Melvin steadied himself and looked around the large back dining room area where the staircase was located. It was silent, almost too silent. This back dining area was used by whatever help his mother employed; it was where they were to eat and take their breaks. Many different housemen and women had run their course in that room over the years; Adele was terrible to work for, and she went through butlers and cooks and the like as if they were disposable. But at the current time, she didn't have anyone caring for her or the home but herself, and of course, Doris was there to be his caregiver. Because of that fact, she was required to break in this room like all the rest. She often sat at the long dining table and did her nursing reports on her computer or ate her meals there, and she constantly listened to soft country and western music on a small old transistor radio which she had brought for herself from her own home. Immediately, Melvin recognized the fact that he heard no faint music at all.

The table was bare. Even when Doris was bustling about the house taking care of other duties which had been outlined by her mother, her computer radio and paperwork remained. Now, though, it was bare, her usual chosen seat tucked neatly back into its spot at the table. It even appeared that the table had been wiped clean at her spot. Where had the woman gone? She was expected to leave only on designated off times; she didn't even sleep at her home at the current time.

"Doris?"

His voice echoed back at him, seeming to circle the room completely. Melvin glanced around at each of the doorways, waiting to see if she came through one of them before he hollered for her again, louder this time.

When he was met with silence yet again, Melvin set his vision on the doorway leading to the main kitchen; she would most likely be in there at this time of day prepping food so she and his mother could prepare his dinner together. Yes, she was likely in there, the radio on a bit too loud for her to hear him.

Crossing the room with jerky movements, Melvin maneuvered his way toward the heavy wood swinging door which led to the large kitchen. He kept his ears peeled, listening for the telltale radio, but as he got closer, all he could hear was a light tapping noise coming from the other room. Finally, he reached the door and put his weight on it gently, opening it; on the other side stood his mother, her back to him. She was humming softly, but he could tell by the way she held herself as she stood there that she knew he was there at the door, watching her.

After several seconds of finishing up what she was doing, Adele turned. She had a small paring knife in her right hand which he could see she had been chopping what appeared to be green onions with. There was a small smile on her face, but it didn't touch her eyes.

"Where have you been, Melvin? I expected you would be resting today while I was gone." She paused long enough to set the knife on the chopping board and reach for a towel on which to wipe her hands. She then continued her voice hardening more and more as she spoke. "But instead, I return early to find myself unable to locate you at all and a nurse who tells me that you wanted to be about the house today, so she let you, against my strict orders. So, where have you been?"

Melvin felt a familiar tremble begin in the pit of his stomach. It moved rapidly, shooting down his legs, and his hands began to shake. Why was he so afraid of his mother? Was it really just her overbearing suffocation? No, there was more, though he couldn't seem to put his finger on the truth in his mind. He was tired of being afraid of her, that much he knew. Just the very thought of Adele Frink made him want to cut her, and the very sound of her voice made him want to smash her skull. The pain in his head was now coming back as the small trace of an itch it had left behind before.

"I was wandering the house," he replied in a low voice, his eyes focusing on hers. With a nervous chuckle, he added, "Guess I wanted to see what all I had really forgotten about the old place."

Adele didn't even flinch. "I would think that you would be much more comfortable in your room, resting. Now, move along, and I'll get your lunch finished and up to you as soon as I can." A smile came to her mouth, and she continued. "Perhaps tonight we can play a game of cribbage or two before I give you your massage and medication." She turned back to the green onions on the cutting board.

"Why would you give me my massage or medications?" Melvin noticed a shift in his mind; something was wrong. "And I don't want to go to my room. I want to see my old study; I have some things I want to go through. Where is Doris?"

Adele stopped slicing as her back and shoulders stiffened. "There is nothing in that study that applies to your life anymore. It's not like you'll be stepping into a physician's career any time soon, wouldn't you agree?"

She made his skin crawl. "Where's Doris?"

Once again, his mother turned around to face him. With a stern voice which challenged him to defy its power, she replied, "Doris really isn't anything for you to worry about either, and for several reasons. For one, she was my employee, not yours. You were simply part of her job description. But since you seem to be so insistent on nosing into business that isn't yours, I sent her home. I sent her home, and she will not be returning. Now, go to your room, change your clothes, and get yourself into bed, Melvin."

He ignored her command. "When will she be back?"

"She won't be!" Spit flew from Adele's mouth, and her face began to redden through her perfect makeup. "The woman was so incompetent that she couldn't even keep a boy as sick as you in his bed. I won't justify my actions to my own child. Now, upstairs!"

Boy? Child? Oh, this woman was the scourge of his life, and she had been for as long as his damaged mind could remember. Melvin had to fight the urge to close the gap between them and strike her so hard with his cane that her head would fly off. But he knew he would never be able to close the gap fast enough, and she would get the better of him. She was a small woman, but something inside of him was bringing back the true facts, making him remember tiny fragments of truth that he had long let go of. If he attempted to get close to her while she was this angry, she would beat him down to the floor before he even realized she had struck. She was the vilest of poisons, the most terrible creature he knew. His soul, if not his mind, was fully aware that this woman took joy in hurting him, and she had done it in all ways possible since the day he had been born.

Adele spoke once again, her voice now nothing more than a stern repetition. "Upstairs, Melvin."

Slowly, Melvin gripped his cane more tightly and turned on his heel. His mind was racing, and his heart was pounding, but he felt no fear. The only emotion he was processing was rage because the very sound of her voice during their interaction had brought it all back to him. No, not all at once, but it brought back enough of a rush of bits and pieces for him to put a few of them together. She had beaten him, and she had beaten him his entire life. As a matter of fact, as he made his way to the lift which she required him to take to keep him weak and limp in her hands, he recalled that she had beaten him terribly the night before his accident. She had taken a switch she had cut from a willow tree in the garden and whipped him about the backside and front, from the waist down, until he had been cut and bleeding, even his privates had been harmed. Yes, she had done that.

He was going to kill her.

Melvin felt her eyes on him all the way through the staff dining area, and even after he passed through one of the swinging doors leading to the main foyer. Without falter, Melvin walked to the lift and pressed the button to call it, and when the door opened almost immediately, he found he was angry. If he had to wait for a moment and she had opened the door to make sure he had gotten on, he would have had the opportunity to turn back and kill her right then and there. But it opened, and he got on it, the rage bubbling inside of him.

Soon he was in his room, almost in a trance, changing into the ugly, striped pajamas she had insisted he always wear. He would have plenty of opportunities to take care of her; he was glad he hadn't snapped. This was going to be the perfect opportunity to get the practice he needed, and that practice would also help him to eliminate the problem of getting the basement ready. When his chance came to take care of her, it would eliminate a lot of things.

For now, he changed into his pajamas and gently placed the small bottles he had brought up from the cellar into the drawer of his nightstand and covered them with a handkerchief. He had everything he needed; chloroform was a definite leg up. He would wait for his supper, tonight, then he would have his massage. It would be while she laid out his pills that he would take the wretched woman down. He would be ready for her.

CHAPTER 5

Dinner turned out to be a light spring salad and grilled chicken breast. Melvin ate it out of sheer hunger; it had no other appeal for him other than that. How he wanted to have a big, bloody steak, baked potato, and a pile of asparagus with melted cheese all over it. Mother would never let him indulge in something like that, but he knew that he would be indulging in much more than that very soon.

It seemed to take forever for time to pass. He stared at the ceiling with a book on his chest most of the time, waiting for his mother to come in and massage him. He hated for her to do it for several reasons, and always preferred Doris' over hers, but he would not be having that tonight. Instead, he would have to endure his mother's hands, which were always too hard on him. She would rub most of his muscles to the point of pain, and it was a pain that he knew would stick with him for hours. But this time, he looked forward to her visit for one small reason: the massage was one step closer to the end of her reign of terror.

∞

Just as he suspected, the massage was a tough one to

handle, and at several points throughout, he thought he was going to reach his breaking point and smash her skull right then or there, but he knew that patience was the best option. Once she left, he had only one hour to wait before she would return and begin to prepare his pills for him, and that was when he would get down to business.

So, Melvin paced the room for nearly that full hour. He let his mind latch onto what he was about to do, and he felt more peace and happiness than he had felt since coming out of his coma. He was excited, almost to a sexual point, at the thought of having this dreadful woman under his thumb once and for all. As he paced and thought, he smiled a smile of pure joy. Before he knew it, it was time.

He went over to his bed and sat down on the edge of it. Reaching into his nightstand, Melvin withdrew one of the small bottles of chloroform from the drawer, along with the handkerchief which had concealed it along with its twin. He swung his legs onto the bed, laid his cane alongside them, then saturated the handkerchief with the chloroform, making sure to keep it far enough away from himself that he wouldn't get dizzy or lightheaded; that wouldn't do. When he was finished, Melvin made himself comfortable and kept one hand under the pillow with the soaked cloth tight in his grasp.

He could hear his own heart pounding in his chest, and the feeling of the nervous adrenaline pumping through his body gave him a chill. He could hear her coming, her short heels clicking on the hardwood floors in the old way that always made him shake.

But tonight, he was shaking with anticipation.

"Hello, Melvin," she greeted as she walked through the door. "How are you feeling after your massage?"

Adele walked over to his dresser and opened the small metal box that held his pills. As she placed each individual dosage out on a doily on a small plate, she tried to chatter with him, at first regarding some senselessness about Dr. Arondale not being able to show up to their lunch, but then she shifted the topic backward. Shooting a glance at him, she asked, with persistence and slight impatience, how he felt after his rub-down.

Melvin shifted his head on his pillow and met his mother's eyes with a steely stare. "Sore. You're too rough on me, and you always have been. I'll be sore until noon tomorrow, and then tomorrow night I'll have to go through it all again. I hope you intend on hiring another nurse soon."

Adele stared back at him, the surprise on her face obvious. Was this her son talking back to her? She studied him, and soon his eyes shifted away from hers. Something was off, and it gave her an unrecognizable chill.

"I didn't know you felt so strongly about it," she replied hesitantly. Adele placed the last pill bottle back into the metal box and secured it, then poured a glass of water from his pitcher and walked to his bed with the medications. Melvin kept his eyes on the wall across the room, but as Adele sat down on the edge of the bed, he let them shift to her for a second. She sat forward to place the water and plate on his nightstand, and that was when he struck.

Melvin's right hand, which had been snugly holding the handkerchief beneath his pillow, suddenly shot out, and as he placed the cloth over her mouth and nose, he quickly sat up and grabbed her around her chest from behind with his left arm. She began to struggle immediately, her legs kicking out, sending practically everything from his nightstand askew. Her eyes were wide, and as he held her small body tightly in his arms, she stared into his eyes; Melvin stared right back, his smile growing as the fear in her eyes grew. He found himself wondering if she could feel his heartbeat because he was sure he could feel hers.

Then it came on her, and her eyes began to flutter, and in only seconds, she was unconscious.

Melvin sat staring at her for a bit. This was the way she should be: silent, with that massive mouth of hers closed. He was going to take care of it. One way or another, she would be the perfect mother.

∞

"Good morning..."

Adele Frink's eyelids fluttered once again, for the first time since being in his bedroom. Something was rousing her... noise... sound.

"I know you're in there. Time to wake up."

She didn't understand the noises and sounds; she was unable to distinguish them as a human voice, and she recognized two words. There were only small, individual sounds, and they were interrupting her from wherever she was. As her eyes tried to blink themselves open, the woman recognized shadows, but she wasn't able to identify them as such. In fact, she was really unaware of any knowledge of anything at all, except her own existence.

"There you go... there you go. Open those eyes."

The light hurt her as she tried to do just that, and her mind raced with utter confusion at the persistent sounds. She looked to the left, then the right, as her vision began to clear a bit. Finally, she looked straight ahead and saw a face, something or someone. The face was familiar, but she had no way of understanding that, nor why it was. All she knew aside from the face before her, she had no idea who she was or where she was.

"Mother," Melvin said as he looked down at her and wondered at her shifting, confused eyes. "You're awake now. I'll give you some rest, but first, I want to show you something."

Melvin disappeared from her view, then returned over her. He was smiling even more now, and she struggled to recall who this person was. The smile brought recognition, but it still evaded her.

"Look what we've done," he said.

Suddenly, Melvin put a hand-held mirror over her face and held it there. Adele looked at her own reflection, confused. Melvin watched her expression with joy; it had worked. She was here, yet she wasn't. He let his eyes drift to gaze at her face entirely. Her upper forehead was now completely bare of any hair except for a few whips he had missed behind her right ear. On her upper forehead were two bloody holes, which he had taken care to properly pack, but he had left the bandages off so she could see. He had to admit that the holes were perfect.

"See, Mother? See the holes? That was where I fixed you. Now you can let go of all of your demons and just be."

She didn't comprehend, he could see that. So, Melvin put down the mirror on the metal table next to him before turning all of his attention to her. He began to gently stroke her head.

"When the hair grows back, this will be much better. Now, try to sleep. When you wake up, your food will be right over there."

Melvin rose with jerky movements, but none of it phased Adele. As he left the room, she simply stared in the direction he had pointed in, not registering the fact that she was looking at a large set of silver dog bowls which sat on a rubber mat on the concrete floor. She simply stared until she drifted off to sleep once again, not knowing the horror her life had become.

CHAPTER 6

Melvin left her lying on the mat on the floor. He didn't leave her in bad shape, though; he made sure she had clean sheets and was covered with a light blanket. He didn't really think it mattered, however; Mother looked as though she was feeling no pain, much less the cold dankness of the basement cell.

After the procedure, which he had performed in one of the first front cells, he had taken the time to tidy up. He hung a picture of his father on the wall after he made up her mat. Next, he placed a five-gallon bucket on the floor and put a toilet seat on top for comfort. He doubted she would be using that, though. At least, not for a while. Melvin expected daily cleanup work for himself for some time.

The final touch to the room had been the dog bowls. The funny thing was, Melvin was actually able to see her as a permanent fixture once he put them down. Now he had a pet, sure, but it wasn't going to do. He wanted much more than something to feed, love, and pet for a companion. His ideal one would be a receptacle for all of his desires. But for now, she would make a nice, quiet little friend.

He pondered the procedure for a bit, then. It had gone so smoothly. Of course, lobotomies weren't performed anymore, so all he had was the strands of book smarts remaining from before his accident, and his actual textbooks, of course. So, armed with those things, he had gone ahead and done it, keeping in mind that she would likely die the entire time. So far, she had not, and this gave him great pleasure. He would much rather have her stunned stupid in his prison than dead in hell.

Melvin had opted for the former. Not only would she be safe and cared for with him, but he would be able to get his act together regarding putting the basement into proper shape. Certainly, it would do for now the way that it was, but he thought he might add some small touches. Perhaps he would replace the mats on the floor with mattresses, not that she, or any other pet he planned to bring home, would know the difference. He also thought he might add music… that may soothe anyone who began to show aggression.

But he was getting ahead of himself, wasn't he? He had only Mother here and hadn't even begun to consider where he would shop for his next little piece of entertainment. All he knew was that the next one was going to be his little toy, his little vessel. The thought made him tingle all over, and he felt that he needed to move. He wanted to get things started as soon as possible.

Back upstairs, Melvin made his way to the employee kitchen, which also housed an exit which led to the garages. He passed through the dining room and through the swinging door before stopping before the exit. Looking at the keys hanging in a long box on the wall, he chose a plain white delivery van, which was used by his mother's first butler at the house. He was in charge of all house shopping, laundering, and other errand activities. The old van was in running order, he was sure. His mother always had all the vehicles serviced regularly, whether they were used or not. Yes, he knew the van was the best choice. He leaned his cane against the cupboard and left it there before grabbing the keys off the hook; it would only get in the way. Besides, he needed to get all of his strength back, not to depend on a wooden stick for the rest of his life.

Just as he suspected, the van started right up, and Melvin spent the next hour purchasing small things for the basement: better blankets, a couple of small pillows, and a small radio. He also stocked up on cans of potted meat and cans of corn and green beans. He would mix the items together, and it would make a soft dish that would provide some kind of nutrition to his little lovelies.

Next, he began to drive around, not aimlessly, but with no solid destination in mind at the same time. He wanted to remind himself of the city, its streets, and its people. It seemed to him that almost all of it had drifted from his mind, except for tiny bits and pieces. Certain stores were still in the same places, particular parks jogged his memory, and there were even specific signs that, for some reason, had stayed the same. Eventually, Melvin drove around enough that he found himself on very familiar ground. He had forgotten how close they lived to Johns Hopkins, and now here he was.

All at once, while sitting at a stoplight, it rushed back to him: school, his studies, and the milling, bustling students who were always rushing around. The pretty girls were everywhere, just as they were when he was there. Just like then, none took notice of the dark-blond, bespectacled man in the white van.

But then one of them did.

She was crossing the street right in front of him, and he would have missed her, if not for the hoot that came from the car next to him. He turned to see who made the noise and why to see a younger man in a dark green truck. The man was smiling and ogling at the girl as she stepped off the curb to cross. Melvin followed his eyes and saw her, and he too became immediately distracted.

She was about five-foot-four, with shoulder-length blond hair that was bouncy and shiny. She had a bounce in her step, as well, and a pert little nose that set her tiny face off perfectly. She turned and looked at the kid in the truck, rolled her eyes, and kept on. But then her eyes went to Melvin, and her face broke out in a grin… she even blushed.

Right away he could envision her with him forever. He thought about the process of making her his own, and his mind began to plan. She would be a perfect start to his little menagerie.

She reached the other side of the street and hoisted a black backpack up onto her shoulder more securely before continuing her trek. Melvin tried to keep his eyes on her, but the car behind him honked loudly, startling him and causing him to press the gas with the jerk of his foot before driving on through the light. He was going to lose her!

Melvin quickly took a right, barely squeezing between oncoming traffic, into one of the campus lots. He quickly turned around, then shot out of the lot at his first opportunity. Soon he could see her walking, oblivious to his presence. He kept a short distance behind, following her just to see where she would go. Melvin knew that he would likely not discover where she lived, or anything else about her. But perhaps he could gain a clue about her routine this way, and that would help matters.

She didn't walk for long. After a couple more blocks, the girl turned and went around a corner, which happened to lead to the Eisenhower Library. Hanging back, he turned the corner and crept the van behind her; she seemed to be in her own world, taking no notice at all of what was going on around her. He wanted to see if she went into the library because if she did, he was more than willing to wait for her to come out. The thought of any care for his mother was now out of his mind.

Going into the library was exactly what the girl did. She entered through one of the main doors, and Melvin set about parking the van in an inconspicuous spot, one where he wouldn't stand out, but could still keep his eyes on the door. He got comfortable and began to wait.

But then it hit him, the exhaustion. He had been up all night, and he had taken no nourishment whatsoever. As he sat, his eyelids slowly began to droop as he nodded off.

Soon, Melvin Frink was in a deep sleep and the girl he had been watching left the library safe and sound, in one piece. She had no idea how close she had come to the end of life as she had known it. But she walked right out of his trap smoothly and quickly, and she was none the wiser to her own near-demise.

∞

Melvin jerked slightly, startled by some sound. It came again, a slight rapping. His eyes fluttered, and he looked around. Where was he?

It was dark, but even so, it began to come back to him. The little blond girl who went into the library. He found the library with his eyes, and he could tell that it was pretty much cleared out. He had missed his opportunity, he was sure. The thought enraged him.

"Sir, do you have a permit for parking?"

Melvin jerked his head toward the voice. A campus police officer stood next to the van with a flashlight in his hand. He looked in on Melvin, shining the light into the van's interior.

"Um, I don't, sir," Melvin replied as he rolled down the window. "I used to be a student, but I had an accident a while back. I guess I was just looking the old place over and I got a bit tired… guess I fell asleep."

The officer studied him. "You look familiar, son."

Melvin shifted his eyes to the man's nametag. It read

"J. Torrey," and Melvin recognized the name immediately. The man had been the first to respond to an on-campus mugging about a week before his accident; he had forgotten the entire incident until that very second, but now the incident came back to him in its entirety. He had been heading home after leaving that very library, and he had witnessed the whole thing, which led to Melvin having to give a police report to the man.

"Officer Torrey," Melvin replied. "I'm Melvin Frink. I had been a student here, and I witnessed a mugging. You probably don't remember, but…"

The large man cut him off. "I do remember you, but not from the mugging. You had an accident like you said. It was horrible, if I recall… in all the papers. How have you been?"

Melvin had done nothing wrong, except for the fact that he didn't have a valid driver's license and he had been stalking a girl. Nonetheless, he felt a twinge of paranoia, and he hoped he could play it off properly. He really wasn't sure what to do except to answer the man's question as lightly and calmly as possible.

"I'm okay, I guess," he replied. "It's been a hard road, but here I am."

The man nodded and smiled, and Melvin felt relief course through his veins. The man had relaxed upon recognizing him, and Melvin thought he stood a good chance of the man not asking for his license. He thought about the girl who had obviously gotten away, and the anger came, but he fought it off and maintained his smile.

Officer Torrey nodded at him. "Well, I should tell you that the campus has had a number of incidents, and I'd encourage you to get yourself home. Unsavory types have been wandering around; I'd hate to think that you might get hurt... again. You know what I mean?"

"Right," Melvin replied as he sat forward to start the ignition. "Guess times have gotten worse instead of better... the people too."

Torrey nodded his head somberly. "Yeah, people especially. Well, you go on now, and take care on your way."

"Thanks, Officer."

Melvin put the van into reverse and backed out of the spot. He was smiling, but on the inside, he was seething with anger at himself. Maybe he should be thankful; maybe he would have been caught if he had tried to get the girl. If the campus cops were out and about so much because of the raised crime rate, well, the campus was likely not the place to be looking.

He pulled out of the lot and took a right. It was nearly ten, according to the clock on the radio, and while that may be the perfect hour to start a good hunt, he had to get back and deal with Mother and the other things at home. He still had his purchases as well. Just thinking about the fact that he had lost track of his game made him squirm in his seat, but he got one thing out of it: he knew what type he was looking for... she had been perfect. It would have been nice if he could have scored her, but it wasn't meant to be.

CHAPTER 7

The rest of the night went by easily enough for him, especially since he had gotten a nap. Mother had been lying in her own feces and urine when he returned, groaning and screeching in his direction. She required a full bath, and Melvin was more than happy to do it. He crooned at her and told her about his day as he cleaned her body, and he took extra time with her face; he knew how she always treated it with care.

Returning to her cell was another story. He had forgotten the mess which she had made, which prompted the bathing, to begin with. It was horrible; not only had she messed her mat, sheets, and blankets, but Mother had managed to smear her own feces all over the wall; it even seemed she might have played with it in some manner. Well, animals would be animals, wouldn't they? At any rate, the sight of Mother's cell prompted him to put plastic garbage bags over her mat before one of the rubber mattress covers he had purchased, then he was able to make the bed properly with bedding. Once the entire job was complete, wall scrubbing and all, he fetched Mother and got her safely tucked in her bedding. He gave another minor attempt at feeding and watering her and was pleased that she took a quarter of his potted meat mixture; she also took water. Once she was finished, Melvin checked to make sure her adult diaper was secure and left her.

But he didn't leave the basement right away. He gave the other cells (or cages, as he had come to fondly think of them) a final look, smiling to himself as he went. On each mat was proper bedding; he had provided each room with makeshift toilets (though he would be cleaning up messes for some time; it would take a while before his pets would be able to go on their own in the toilet), and matching sets of dog dishes in each. Eighties big hair rock played softly from the end of the hall, and he bounced his head to an old Cinderella song.

∞

He was exhausted. It hit him hard as soon as he closed the door to the basement behind him after he left. Melvin leaned back against it and took a long, ragged breath. Tiny beads of sweat dampened his forehead, and he was panting slightly, but he felt good. He glanced down at his watch and was pleased to see that it was now eight-thirty in the morning... perfect! He would grab a sandwich, sleep for a few hours in the parlor on the sofa, and then he would get up and go look for his little friend.

The thought of her hadn't left his mind. He remembered the exact color of her hair and the way her nose crinkled when she had smiled at him. If he didn't know better, he would have sworn he could remember her smell, though logic and reason (what he had left of it, anyway) told him that was not possible. But it was how he knew she was to be the first one: she never left his mind... and he couldn't wait to taste her.

In the parlor, Melvin sat on the sofa, chewed slowly on the first bite of his tuna melt, and held a single potato chip, forgotten, in his right hand. He stared at the television as though engrossed by a program, but the volume was muted, and he wasn't registering the television's existence in the slightest. Rather, Melvin was thinking about how he had set his watch for two in the afternoon, and how he would go back to where he first saw her at the light. He doubted she would be there, but he planned to park somewhere and hang out, just in case.

After a while, if she didn't show, he would go to the Eisenhower Library and wait. He would likely do this every day until she finally came; after all, she was bound to come sometime. He was a firm believer that persistence paid off.

He finished his sandwich and chips, then washed them down with cold milk before stretching and making himself comfortable. An Afghan his grandmother had knitted when he was young was draped over the back of the sofa, so he grabbed it and covered himself with it. Melvin used a throw pillow to support his head.

Within only seconds, Melvin Frink was snoring soundly.

∞

Melvin was dreaming.

The girl was right there, right on the corner, right in front of him. It was just like when he first saw her, except everything was in slow motion, and the guy in the car next to him was driving a red Ferrari and had horn stubs growing out of his forehead. He was staring at Melvin and chuckling. He would motion toward the cute blond with his head and lick his lips.

Melvin's eyes went to the blond. She was crossing now, and they made eye contact. Just like before, she smiled the sweetest smile, and Melvin thought his heart might beat through his chest. He pressed the accelerator without a second thought and ran her over.

Suddenly, Melvin was in the basement, and Gorgeous Blond was wearing a spiked leather collar and was chained to the wall. Her bangs were gone, and there were two little holes where Melvin had made her his own. He was inside of her, pounding and grinding, staring at the holes with rising arousal. Spit trickled from the corner of her mouth and dripped toward the ground, where it made a tiny pool. All she did was a grunt.

Then, his mother yelled from the other cage, "Girls are dirty, Melvin; I've always told you that. Now put her down and come to wipe my ass, you filthy boy!!"

∞

Melvin shot up from where he was sleeping on the couch, his eyes wide, his body sweaty. As soon as he realized that he was home, that it had been a dream, he shoved his hand down his sweatpants and began to vigorously abuse himself. He thought about the little blond while he did it, and it was only seconds until the job was done.

Afterward, Melvin lay spent, panting and gasping, sweat dripping from him. His eyes were closed, and he replayed the scene over and over in his mind. It took him ten minutes just to come back down to Earth and begin to think straight. He grabbed his watch from the cocktail table and squinted at it: it was only ten in the morning. He had to get more sleep, or nothing would work out as planned. He wasn't in the best shape of his life, and as far as getting stronger, well, he had a long way to go.

Slowly but surely, he dozed and then slept, fading thoughts of his new toy lingering in his mind. He would have her, or he would search for her forever. But he wasn't one to lie to himself, either.

If it took too long, he would definitely be acquiring others during his search, and his search started today.

∞

Melvin yawned. He had been sitting in his van in the parking lot of some student apartments that sat at the intersection where he had first seen her, the one at the stop light. He had been there for three hours, a bit later than the last time, but he had to wing it with the information he had, long-shot or not.

Reaching over to the passenger seat, Melvin grabbed up a candy bar and tore open the wrapper. He began to eat it, tearing into it and chewing, but not really tasting it at all. About halfway through it, he took a swig off a now-cold coffee and winced. Time for a store run.

He started the van and glanced first out the rearview mirror on the ceiling: clear. Shifting his eyes, he looked out the one on his door, then the one on the passenger door.

And there she was.

She was approaching the van from behind, the same black backpack slung from her left shoulder. A light breeze blew through her blonde hair, and she was looking up at the sky with a smile on her face. For Melvin, it was like a dream... too good to be true. He never thought that he would see her again at all; he especially didn't think that he would have an opportunity to take her home on his very first day out. But here she was, nonetheless, approaching his van on her own. He would hardly have to do a thing, and she would be his.

Very quickly, Melvin scrambled for his vial of chloroform and clean hanky. He began to pour the liquid onto the cloth with trembling hands, his eyes glued to her reflection in the rearview mirror. He almost dropped the bottle and spilled its contents, but just in time, he was able to catch it. He corked it, tucked it in the console, and got out of the van fast. As he rounded the rear of the vehicle, Melvin came face to face with her.

"Excuse me?"

She stopped and looked at him, smiling; wow, she was an angel! She couldn't be more perfect. He was almost frozen in place as he gazed upon her beauty.

"Can I help you?" she asked.

Melvin had to struggle to gain his bearings. "Um, actually, I'm lost." He fiddled with the hanky in his pocket. "I don't have one of those GPS things... well, I don't even have a cell phone, believe it or not. Anyway, I have this map of the campus, and I am having the hardest time reading it."

Her smile faded quite a bit, and suspicion came over her face. "Well, I don't know..."

Melvin chuckled shyly and blushed. He looked at the ground and began to kick a rock around with his foot. "Listen, I understand. This day and age, you can never be sure about people, right?"

"Right." She looked around the lot, and he followed suit; there was no one in sight. "Maybe you could grab the map and bring it to me, and then I could help a bit."

"Good idea," he replied with a smile. "Oh, by the way, I'm Mel... Mel Collins. I'll be right back."

He made his way to the van and opened the passenger door. He rummaged around in the glove box until he fished out a small stack of papers that were stapled at one corner; it appeared to be an old inventory list from the house supplies. It would do. He turned to go back to the girl.

"I'm Sarah Russell," she told him as he neared. "Sorry for the apprehension; it's just that there have been a lot of crimes and stuff on campus. I guess I'm just wary. You look safe enough, I must say."

Melvin nodded. "I understand, believe me. I'm just getting back on my feet after a coma, so I'm a bit behind technology-wise, hence the paper map. Anyway,

I sure appreciate your help." Melvin handed her the map and stood slightly behind her, letting his eyes roam over the lot; they were completely alone.

"Um, Mel... this is some kind of grocery list or something."

Sarah Russell no sooner got the words out of her mouth than he came at her. His right arm went around her and covered her nose and mouth with the chloroform-soaked hanky, and his left arm grabbed her around her midsection, lifting her off the ground. She kicked only a handful of times before going limp, and Melvin had no problem putting her into his van. The passenger side door was already open, so he put her in the seat and buckled her in securely and reclined it just a bit. Then he fetched her backpack, which she had dropped during the struggle. With the bag in hand, he jumped in the driver's seat, tossed the pack into the rear, started the engine, and calmly put the van into gear. He smiled and hummed to himself as he made his way out of the lot and steered the vehicle back home.

As he drove, he looked over at her. She was wonderful, everything he had ever imagined his first real pet would be. Now it was important to get her to the house and get her downstairs. There, he would strap her to a table, maintain her level of unconsciousness, and then he would carry out the procedure. He intended to eliminate every ounce of a fight she had left in her, and he would do it quickly and efficiently.

But he wouldn't care for her the way he did for Mother, because she was special. He made sure to meet

Mother's basic needs, and sure, he gave her a bit of attention now and then, but nothing like the attention he was going to give to little Miss Sarah Russell. She was going to be different. For one thing, he wasn't going to do too much when he severed her frontal cortex. He was going to leave a bit of Sarah Russell in the shell because he wanted her to realize that she had a master who loved her to no end. He wanted her to show expression on her face when he was ravaging her, day after day, as he planned to do. He remembered his dream from earlier that day, and he grew hard in his pants. It was uncomfortable, and he needed relief soon. So, when he pulled the van into the gates back at the house and parked it in its proper space, he reached over and shoved his hand in her blouse and under her bra. He unbuttoned and unzipped his jeans with his other hand, then proceeded to relieve himself as quickly as possible. Sarah Russell began to moan lightly, and he had to re-dose her just to keep her out and get her in the house.

Thirty minutes later, Melvin had her strapped down to one of the metal tables in the basement. She had the largest "cage," one in the very rear, as far from his mother as possible. He made sure she was completely unconscious before going to tend to Mother. It was important to keep her cleaned up and fed, if at all possible.

But Mother didn't look so good. Not only had she urinated all over herself and was developing sores on her right hip and shoulder. She was also the color of wet concrete and appeared to not have any idea what was going on. He changed her bedding, gave her a quick sponge bath, and put a clean gown on her before trying to spoon-feed potted meat into her mouth. She spit out most of it, but got down a bit, along with a few sips of water. Mother also made almost no sound at all, and Melvin could tell that she had gained no recognition of him nor her surroundings. He had a feeling deep inside that the thing with Mother wasn't going to end well. But for now, he would care for her as best as he could.

Now it was time to tend to Sarah. He prepared all of his supplies on a metal table, washed his hands thoroughly and obsessively, then cut her bangs off and covered the rest of her hair with a surgical cap. When he had prepared himself and her fully, he picked up his drill and smiled down at her.

"You're going to be better," he said to her. "I am going to tread a bit more lightly with you, my love. By the time a few days pass, you will not only begin to show recognition and conscious thought, but you will also be at my beck and call, my little pet."

With his smile frozen in place, Melvin turned on the drill and aimed the small bit at the first iodine covered dot on her upper forehead. He paused only briefly to check the anesthesia before moving forward.

Soon, tiny bits of bone and dust were flying.

CHAPTER 8

Melvin woke shortly before six the following evening. Unbelievably, the first thing on his mind was Mother; it was as if he had forgotten all about Sarah Russell and her surgery. He sat on the edge of his bed rubbing his eyes for a full three minutes before it struck him. Sarah Russell, the cute little blonde he had been targeting as his pet, was in the last cage in the basement waiting for him.

Without a second thought, Melvin stood up and limped his way across his massive room to the heavy door which enclosed it. He flung open the door and made his way to the lift, not willing to try and take the stairs. He needed to get to her as soon as possible. The surgery that he had done on her had ended at two in the morning, and here he had been sleeping pretty much ever since. Fear filled his heart, and his hands trembled; what if she was dead down there? What if he had gone to all of the trouble to acquire all of her perfection and beauty only to let it rot and die? The very thought made him sick to his stomach, and he thought that he might not make it to the basement before passing out from nausea.

When finally the lift door opened, Melvin rushed out of the door as fast as he could and made his way across the area leading to the basement door and the set of steps which led down to it. He took the steps two at a time, nearly tumbling to the landing at the bottom on more than one occasion. He flung open the door and rushed inside as fast as his gimpy legs could carry him. He gave his mother's cage nothing more than a glance. She was gurgling slightly and trying to look around the room, her skin was pastier than before. But none of that even distracted him from the concern he felt for Sarah Russell in the last cage.

Then he was there, the door opened with the allowed creak. Sarah Russell was lying on the mat on the floor covered in a thick comforter. Through the gauze on her head, where he had drilled holes were tiny spots of blood, but nothing more. There was no leakage or any type of pus or drainage that he could see.

Her eyes had been closed, of that much he was sure. But now, as he neared her slowly and with jerky movements, he saw that they were slowly opening. She was staring straight at him as he approached, but her eyes were obviously out of focus, and Melvin knew that there was no recognition of him in her eyes. He was about three feet away from her when her lip started to move. Melvin froze in place, his eyes widening in surprise.

"M-M Mel…" A stringer of drool fell to the floor from the corner of her mouth.

"M-M…"

Melvin was stunned… he had told her his name was Mel. She was in good shape. He closed the short gap between them and smiled as he knelt next to the mat she was on. Melvin studied her with pleasure before glancing around to see if she'd made any kind of mess… she really had not. Nothing to speak of anyway.

"You remember me?" Melvin reached out and began to stroke her hair. Trying to nod, she suddenly winced, as if in pain, her left eye blinking rapidly.

"Are you in pain, Sarah? Does your headache?"

Now her attempt at nodding was much clearer and more persistent. Melvin rose immediately. He couldn't have any fun if her head ached. He wanted her to focus on what he would be doing to her, not her head. Yes, he wanted her to feel a wonderful pain only he could give.

Melvin rushed down the hall to the small supply room, where he had spotted a small, outdated box containing packets of aspirin. They were expired, so he grabbed two packets of two each. He thought about the fact that they could cause problems by thinning her blood, but as old as they were, he didn't let the thought linger. They would have to do for now; later he would raid Mother's medicine cabinet; there was surely something more effective there.

He reached Sarah's cell and poured her a small cup of cold water from a pitcher he had prepared beforehand. Picking it up, he looked down at her, lying there on her mat; the sight first entranced him.

Sarah hadn't stopped squirming and groaning since she had woken, and she had managed to get her gown twisted around her waist, and she was fully exposed, her kicking legs splashing out and revealing her fully to him. Melvin was nearly smacking his lips, her groaning unheard and the aspirin was forgotten.

Melvin's member began to throb, and his hand started trembling, causing drops of water to leap from the small cup and land on the cold concrete floor. His eyes began to travel slowly up the length of her body, the sight of her saturating his mind entirely. Melvin forgot all about the packets of aspirin and the water, even dropping them onto the floor. But then his eyes met hers, and he knew that something was very different this time around.

Sarah was still squirming around on her mat, her gown twisted even higher, as it was now bunched up under her breasts. She was looking directly into his eyes, unflinching and without fear. The girl was still groaning and gurgling, her mouth moving rapidly as though she were speaking and telling him some great lecture or angry story, but not an understandable word came out. All that Melvin was aware of was her eyes, however. Sarah looked scared, but more than anything, she looked extremely pissed off. Her anger did nothing for him; he couldn't care less about that. But that fear... that fear was turning him on.

Her possible headache was no longer of any concern to him whatsoever. Melvin simply strode over to where she lay, dropping his jeans and boxers as he went. He was able to note the exact moment she registered his intent: her anger disappeared entirely and in its place came horror, but the procedure he had performed had made it impossible, at least for the time being, for her to articulate it. Sarah opened her mouth and screamed as she struggled to get away from him.

But there was nowhere for her to go. Melvin was on her like a bird landing on its prey. He grabbed her by the arm and flung her over onto her stomach, the concern he had shown her only moments before now completely untraceable in his behavior. Sarah tried to fight, but she was so weak, and Melvin, for all of his post-accident weakness, seemed so strong.

Her scream continued as he thrust himself forcefully into her. Her shrieks of terror soon emitted obvious pain, and then, as he let go inside of her, the unintelligible cries of pain dwindled to nothing more than sobs of dismay, shame, and disgust.

He collapsed on top of her then, immediately drained like never before in his life. For a full five minutes, he was gasping for breath but was finally able to breathe almost normally again. It was then that he realized his mother was screaming at the top of her lungs from her own cell. He sat on the edge of the mat and smiled; it was the most promise she had shown since he had taken her mind from her.

Then Sarah's sobs came to his ears once again, and a wave of disgust came over him. Disgust at himself for some reason he couldn't understand, but mostly disgust with Sarah Russell for hating what they had just done together in such an obvious manner. She should have been thanking him.

"Shut up," he said softly as he reached for his boxers and began to pull them on. When she didn't stop immediately, he became almost enraged and slapped her hard in the back of her head. "I said shut up!"

Sarah turned her head away from him and buried her face in the blanket, but the sobs continued to wrack her body. Melvin watched her cry for a moment but felt no sadness. The only thing he felt was a slight sense of frustration at her lack of appreciation. He reached out and began to stroke the hair at the back of her head, much the way one would pet their dog. He clucked his tongue and shook his head in the most sympathetic manner he could muster, and when he spoke, he spoke gently. He certainly wouldn't want his little pet to hate him. In the end, he intended for her eyes to be opened to all he was doing for her, for them both, and then she would be able to happily obey his every wish and command. Patience was vital.

"Now, now," he crooned, and as soon as the words left his mouth, his mother stopped screaming, much to his relief. "Is it really that bad for your master to show you how much he loves you? I have done so much for you, and for myself, by bringing you here. I have freed you from the prison of yourself and brought you here to care for you. How could you not desire my touch? You'll get used to it, I promise."

Melvin stood and pulled on his jeans, then crossed the room and grabbed a towel from a stack he had placed on the metal table next to the cups, water pitcher, and an empty basin. He then filled the basin with the water, which was chilled to room temperature; he was sure she wouldn't mind. Then he returned to her and began to clean her up, even washing her face gently and wiping the tears away. Sarah kept her eyes shifted away from him the entire time, but he refused to take note of it. Continuing to feed her words of encouragement, he then straightened her gown and tucked her beneath her blankets before giving her the aspirin he had fetched and promised her something stronger next time. Finally, he moved the plastic mat with the dog dishes closer to her bed and offered her some, but Sarah clamped her mouth tightly closed and turned her head away.

"That's fine," he told her. "But you will need to eat, you know. It is important for you to keep up your strength. That's why fighting me is so counter-productive. You want to be happy and healthy, don't you? Well, I am just the one to make that happen, if you listen to me and obey."

He leaned down to kiss her cheek and give her head another stroke. "Now sleep. I need to tend to Mother."

With that and a smile on his face, Melvin rose and left her cell, making sure the door was secured and locked behind him. As he took the few steps to his mother's cell, he hummed, happy and content, as if he hadn't just raped, kidnapped and crudely lobotomized a woman.

On the contrary, Melvin felt that everything was perfect in his world for the first time in a long, long time.

CHAPTER 9

It was nearly midnight, and Melvin was in the main living area on the sofa writing in a spiral notebook which served as his journal. His feet were on the cocktail table, bent at the knees, propping the notebook up for him, and his head was bent over, hair spilling into his eyes as he furiously scratched away with a cheap pen; they always had been his favorite, especially in red, as this one was. The TV softly played in the background; he had tuned it to some forensics cop show thinking that now was a good time to try and learn some of their tricks, but it didn't take him long to figure out that the program was a trumped-up bunch of malarkey. That was when he began to document the day's events, as he had been doing every day of his life since he had been capable of writing. Well, except for the time spent in his coma, of course. Thanks to the journal, the cop show was nothing more than noise for him, which he welcomed.

His brain had been itching badly off and on for most of the day. Most people would have likely categorized it as a sharp pain, he guessed, but for him, it was an itch that he couldn't scratch no matter how hard he tried. It always came on in a sharp, stinging manner, but as time wore on it generally lessened to the nagging itch he now felt. Every now and then his hand would subconsciously go to his forehead, to that spot just over his eye, and he would scratch at the skin. It never did any good. The only thing that helped was to try to keep his mind off of it until bedtime when sleep would mercifully ease it for him.

As he wrote, he carefully considered the day's events and the state of the household with each word he put on paper. He had tried to give Mother her meals, but she had seemed to be in a steady state of catatonia which, until his lovemaking session with Sarah, had appeared to be getting worse. Melvin figured he had done too much to her during the procedure, and until her deafening screams had come to believe she would likely die eventually. Now he wasn't so sure. When he went to check on her after leaving Sarah's cell, she still had something of a blank look on her face, but now there was a pinpoint of recognition and rage deep within them. She had stared at him when he opened the door, and even though she seemed to be looking right through him, Melvin could have sworn he felt rage and chastisement coming out of them and permeating her entire being. There was no way she could possibly know what had been done to her, or what he was up to now, just no way. Or was there? Was it possible that she was slowly, but surely, gaining back some of her capacities? It was a nice thought. After all, he never intended to end her life. Even though he had endured a lifetime of abuse at her hands behind the closed doors of the fortress they lived in, he loved her dearly. She simply needed to be gotten control of, and it appeared he had gained that control quite nicely.

But all things were trial and error, and it was during his mother's procedure that prompted him to ease up a bit when he did Sarah's; it seemed to work beautifully. The only problem he saw was that Sarah seemed a little bit too strong and aware, as though he had gone from one extreme to the next when it came to the amount he removed from the holes in their skulls. Sarah not only recognized and somehow remembered him, but she also appeared to be recalling the name he had given her when they met. At least, that was what he suspected she had been trying to say, but she had not been able to make her lips form the word, or any other, for that matter. Loss of coordination and muscle control was typical in patients recovering from lobotomization, he knew, and he should... he had been reading up on the subject for years. It always intrigued him; in fact, it was what had prompted him to study psychiatric medicine in the first place. He had longed to find a way to perfect what he had always considered being the right idea that had simply come way ahead of its time. He had believed that even though the procedure was no longer performed, having been forsaken in the light of the modern medicine age, he would someday find a proper and highly-effective way to carry it out. The only difference between the past and the present was that before his accident, Melvin wanted to do it to free the patient of the demons of mental illness; now he simply did it for himself.

As he scribbled all of this in his notebook, it caused him to wonder about the brain matter even more. It appeared that an amount measured directly between the two that he had already attained would be perfect. Of course, there was no way of knowing that without trying...

He needed another girl. This time, he told himself, he would find one solely to perfect the science. Deep inside, though, the very thought of adding to his fledgling collection made his member tingle. He could justify it all he wanted with "science"; the fact was, he was hooked, and he knew it.

Maybe a redhead this time, he thought.

He finished up writing and rose off the sofa, giving his body a long stretch as he did so. Melvin was starving, and he realized that he hadn't eaten. Here, he had been lecturing his little Sarah about the perils of not eating, and he was neglecting his own nourishment. With a chuckle and a shake of his head, Melvin made his way to the kitchen. It was too late to cook much, so he decided on a can of beef stew, heated to perfection. His mother would have gone nuts if she thought he was eating something as hideous as canned stew, or anything else out of a can, for that matter. She would have lost her mind if she had known, and these facts made his mouth water for it all the more.

Ten minutes later, he was back on the sofa with a large bowl of the stew, two slices of buttered wheat bread, and a large, cold glass of milk. He ate slowly and purposefully, enjoying the flavor of the food as he chewed. Content, he let his mind turn back to the calculated amounts and where he would find his next little companion, the one who would sample his updated "solution for the brain," as he liked to think of it. He would need to plan, and that meant he would need to figure out where he was going to start searching for her, and when.

Melvin thought he would spend the day with his two girls, making sure they were alright, clean, and happy first. That meant they were to eat, no matter what. If they refused, he would threaten to start feeding them with a tube; that strategy would likely work on Sarah because she seemed to have some presence of mind about her. He wasn't sure how Mother would react because he was unsure of her true state. Before he had thought she would likely die, but when he checked them for the last time around ten-thirty, Mother had been lying on her back under her blanket. She had been staring at the ceiling, and it sounded like she was trying to sing a song of some sort. There were no words, of course, but there was an obvious lilt to the sounds she was making, and Melvin just knew she was singing. It was beginning to look to him like she might pull through after all. It was going to be fun subjecting her to the sound of him having intercourse with his pets whenever he desired. Had she been herself, she would have burned the head of his member with a cigarette for having sex at all. She forbade anything to take her baby boy from her, especially some dirty streetwalker who had let herself be snatched up off the street, as his Sarah had. In his mother's mind, Sarah had likely lured him to it, but he knew differently. Sarah, like all of them, simply didn't know what was good for her; it was his responsibility to show her. It was his responsibility to show them all... all of them he could get, anyway.

And Melvin Frink knew right then that this was only the beginning; it was never going to stop.

So, where to get his next pet? He considered the campus at Johns Hopkins, which would be a simple choice. College girls, intelligent and gifted or not, seemed to still be naive enough to trust, which surprised him, considering the day and age they were all living in. He couldn't trust his own mother. How were these girls willing to even look at strangers, much less accompany one to a big, white, windowless van to look at a map?

Yes, perhaps Johns Hopkins would be good for one more go around, but he was sure that it wasn't going to be cool to hit the campus for another after that. College campuses were much like small towns. Once the word got out that girls were disappearing everyone would have their eyes out for the likes of him, and he couldn't have that. After all, he was trying to build a family here, so he needed to play it safe.

Yes, he would spend the day with Mother and his Sarah, then when they were bathed, fed, and put down for the night, Melvin would go back to the campus. It would be Friday so he wouldn't have to worry about there being a lack of prospects. They would be milling around like flies, and even if the campus were a bit dead, the local nightlife would be hopping.

With that, he sopped up some of the stew's remaining gravy-like substance out of the bowl with the last bit of his wheat bread and washed it down with the rest of his milk. He didn't bother to take his dirty dishes to the kitchen; Melvin simply piled them up on the end table alongside the sofa with about twelve other unwashed kitchen items. He made a mental note to get motivated and clean up the living area; it was beginning to smell like rotting food and sweat.

∞

With all of these thoughts circling in his mind, and then some, Melvin Frink lay down on the sofa, covered up with his afghan, and turned the television to a late-night talk show; he even turned up the volume, but that had been a waste of time. Within ninety seconds, he was snoring softly, and the beginnings of a dream were creeping up on the edges of his mind.

It was dark out, and a redhead with a small build and big breasts was standing beneath a streetlight on a campus corner, just baiting him...

CHAPTER 10

Contrary to Melvin's mental forecast and emotional bracing, the next day went very easily for him regarding his mother and Sarah Russell. Both were very cooperative in most all of his caretaking, with the exception of eating. It occurred to him, they may simply be refusing the wet food that he had been bowling up for them. He made a special trip in his mother's sedan to the grocery store, where he purchased around fifty jars of various baby foods, all pureed, all chunk-free. He thought he would add a bit of seasoning to make it more appealing, as well as adding small sprigs of parsley just to jazz the servings up a bit. He also made it a point to purchase a nice red merlot, his mother's personal favorite. Hopefully, Sarah would like it as well, and the women may find that it served as a much better "sleeping pill" than the hard-core pain meds his mother had successfully stockpiled in her medicine cabinet, which was almost the size of a kitchen pantry, by the way. He made sure to put individual doses of the pain meds in cups, but opening the wine gave him a sense of satisfaction and peace that he didn't get from pills alone. No, now he was sure that the beauties would both be asleep in no time, and if it weren't for his plan to seek out his next pet, he would have stayed and tried Sarah out while she was out of it. But, however, finding the next member of his family was far more important. He put all the thoughts out of his mind and focused on feeding them, bathing them, and giving them their new food; both his precious babies seemed much more receptive to the food than before. Soon, both his mother and his beloved Sarah were warm, safe, and clean beneath their blankets. He took care of Mother first then went in to tend to Sarah.

Sarah was a lot more receptive to him this time, though she wouldn't look at him at all. Melvin didn't care; he simply moved forward with what needed to be done, giving her a warm sponge bath (which he enjoyed thoroughly, though she looked as though she were holding back tears through the entire thing), giving her food (which she seemed to choke down, and took only three bites of), and finally tucking her in. He sat on the edge of her mat and petted the back of her head, talking to her softly for about ten minutes after that.

"I know you think I'm mean," he crooned, "a terrible human being. But I'm really not. The truth is, you belong here, just like this, just the way you are. It's important for you to realize that. You're my little pet, and now you'll be cared for properly for the rest of your life." Melvin paused, a look of sudden surprised realization coming over his face. "You know, since you now belong to me, and I'm your new family, I think you need a new name. Sarah is nice, but you have a new life now. Let's see..."

His voice dwindled off as he began to think about the topic. Sarah's eyes, which had been focused on an invisible point straight ahead, now shifted slightly in his direction, but quickly returned to their original position. The guy was not only violent, but he was also stark-raving mad. She couldn't put it into words yet, but she had an odd visual in her mind which broke down what she was thinking... he was as nuts as they come.

"Princess!" he shouted then got a startled look on his face and shifted his eyes to the wall in the direction of his mother's cell. "I'd better keep my voice down; wouldn't want to wake Mother, now would we? She's been a bit of a handful for the last couple of days. I wasn't sure she was going to make it, but since I brought you, she seems to be recuperating at last. Slow but sure, they say."

Melvin continued to stroke her hair, his attention fully on her once again. "Yes, Princess is perfect, because you are my little princess. You'll see, Princess: I'm going to give you the very best care and everything you could need or want. You'll love me before it's over."

Sarah's stomach turned uneasily as he leaned down and kissed her temple; his very touch made her want to vomit violently. He wasn't only sick, he was sickening, as well. He had forced her to have sex like she was nothing but a toy. He had taken her away from... from where? She wasn't sure, but she knew she wasn't supposed to be here.

Melvin stood and smiled down at her. "Now, Princess, you get a good night's sleep. I'm going to think of a new name for Mother. You know, her name has always been Adele, but I hate that name... it's cold, hard, and mean, just like her. I think she needs a name that is more suited to her new... personality, don't you?"

With a wink, he made his way out of the cell and locked the door behind him. Sarah waited until she heard the heavy door close, the door she assumed was the only thing between her and the world from which he had taken her. She was determined; when she was able, she would find that door, and she would go through it, and she would go back to where she came from. But first, her mind had to clear up a bit more. She had to be strong enough to get the job done, because Mel, or whatever his name was, wasn't going to make it easy. Of that much she was sure.

She was also sure that when she finally did leave this place, she was going to leave his bloody corpse there as well.

∞

Melvin drove cautiously around the campus, making random turns here and there, making sure he kept the van at the speed limit and obeyed all the traffic signs and lights. Getting pulled over, for any reason, would very well be the end of him. They would try to call his mother because the van was in her name, and he didn't have a license. When they couldn't get ahold of her, they would proceed to take him home in a squad car to speak with her, and all of this because of the stupid license thing, not to mention his supposed brain injury. What they would find at the house would end him, totally and completely, and he wasn't about to let that happen.

He was also concerned about campus police officer John Torrey. The man had been kind, but Melvin knew that kindness would only exist as long as he didn't appear suspicious. That was why it was so imperative that he go to the other side of the campus for his next pet. It was likely that the Eisenhower Library area was Torrey's regular beat, so to return was simply stupid. An ex-student driving around in a white van, especially when a girl had recently disappeared from the campus, would be a certain cause for investigation. For all Melvin knew, the girl had already been reported missing, and Torrey had already brought up the man in the white van sleeping outside of the library. Maybe the van wasn't such a good idea after all.

So, he began to wind his way around to the other side of the campus. He knew of some women's dorms over there that might be the perfect area to hunt; this time of the evening, the girls would be getting ready to go out and have a good time, or meet their boyfriends for dinner, or whatever it was that girls liked to do on a Friday night.

His heart was pounding, and his hands had a slight tremor to them. Yes, he had overthought things for sure. Now he had himself all nervous over returning to the campus to hunt at all. Maybe he should have gone to the lower end of town, where missing girls wouldn't be noticed right away, and neither would suspicious white vans. As he took a right toward the dorms, he decided that he might as well get a good look around while he was here; if nothing panned out, he was going to leave and head where the prospects were safer.

There she was then, just like that. She wasn't a redhead, as he had hoped for, but she was alone, and she was all dressed up and crossing the dorm lot, supposedly heading for her vehicle. Melvin slowed down and, steering awkwardly with his knee, began to soak a hanky with chloroform. He emptied the vial and tossed it behind him into the van's cargo space. Then he took a deep breath. She was right in front of him, walking a bit briskly, looking at something to her right. It was as if she hadn't yet noticed him at all.

Melvin stopped the van about eight or ten feet in front of her and opened the door and jumped out. She noticed him then and stopped. The look on her face was not just cautious, it was almost fearful.

He held up his free hand, his other holding the hanky in his jeans pocket, and smiled. "Hi. I don't mean to scare you. I'm looking for the Eisenhower Library. I'm supposed to pick up a friend there, and it looks like I'm really lost."

The look on her face softened immediately. "Yeah, you are. That's clear on the other side of campus." The girl began walking toward him, a small smile on her face. "This is a pretty big place; it's easy to get lost if you don't know where you're going. I'll explain how to get there."

"Thanks."

As she neared him, she stepped into one of the overhead parking lot lights, and Melvin could see that while her hair wasn't really red, it did have a significant amount of red in it; she was auburn if anything. The lights brought out the red highlights beautifully, and the sight made his heart skip a beat. She was also slender, with smaller breasts, though she was by no means flat-chested. When she smiled at him, he could see that her teeth were white and perfect. He would name her Candy, he thought to himself.

"Okay," she said, pointing a finger toward the mouth of the lot, "you are going to want to take a left out of the lot and go down to the third stop light."

Melvin stepped behind her and looked in the direction she was pointing; she didn't even seem to notice.

"At the light, there will be a gas station on the right; you want to turn left there, then take your first right." The girl turned to him, still smiling. "Are you getting all of this?"

"Perfectly."

She turned again, and this time held up her left hand, the look on her face was slightly distant as she pictured the places she was talking about. "After that, you want to go to Lincoln Avenue and..."

Melvin's arm swooped around her and put the cloth over her mouth and nose, just as he had done with Princess. His left arm went around her stomach, and he lifted her off the ground, kicking and trying to bite at the cloth with her teeth.

"You shouldn't do that," he grunted as he rushed to the van, noting how light she was. "The chemicals will make you sick if you ingest them."

Before he even made it to the open driver's door, she was out. He put her in, got his breath, then stood on the running board and climbed on to the driver's seat, and slowly began to drive around and out of the lot. He took note of his surroundings; it seemed he had chosen the right time to hunt because he didn't see a soul in sight who would have noticed what had just taken place.

Melvin maneuvered his way from the campus to his home, humming as he went, but making sure to keep one eye on the rearview mirror, just in case he was mistaken about having been seen. He was still nervous, no matter how blasé he chose to act, and it wasn't until he had the van pulled up next to the back service and delivery entrance of the house that he truly felt safe and secure. He found himself more thankful than ever for the large wall and main gate, which surrounded the property. When he was younger he had hated them; he felt sure they were there just to keep him in, even though they had been in place for years. Now he knew they were there for the safety of the people and things within.

He put the girl on a stretcher that he had brought in from the old mortuary storage garage. He kept it just inside the service entrance for this purpose, and as he parked the van back in the garage, he mentally patted himself on the back for his forethought.

Soon, Melvin Frink was making his way through the darkness back to the house. He would need coffee and lots of it. It was going to be a long night if he was going to complete another procedure. He would first take her down to a cell he had prepared earlier in the day and make her comfortable until he had some coffee in him and was able to move ahead with her surgery.

Once he was in the kitchen, his mind turned to the stockpile of pills and other controlled substances his mother had stashed in her room. Obviously, she had been getting it all from Dr. Arondale, and had, more than likely, been doing so for years. What was she doing for the doctor, besides giving him money, to entice him into going against his professional ethics and doctor's creed by prescribing such addictive substances? He thought he knew, but he brushed the thoughts from his mind. She was a conniving woman, and she always had been. If not for him, she would likely have remained that way for the rest of her life.

But no more, and she had him and him alone to thank for that.

CHAPTER 11

Campus police officer Sergeant John Torrey hung up the phone on his desk and finished making his notes about the call. It had been from Bradford Willis; his daughter was a student there at Johns Hopkins, studying Genetics and Genetic Research. She hadn't answered her phone for the last day-and-a-half; this was unusual because she typically spoke to her mother twice a day. Her parents were sick with worry and grief, and understandably so. Torrey himself was feeling something like vomit building up in the back of his throat. Jennifer Willis was only one reason. Only a couple of days before, a student named Sarah Russell had been reported missing by her campus apartment roommate. Torrey, who had been working the beat for the last couple of months to help tone down campus crime, had been pulled from the streets to lead the missing person case; now it looked like he would be working two of them.

He finished up his notes and headed into the chief's office, apprehension filling his guts. Something was telling him that this was far more than a couple of girls biding their time until their hangovers passed. These were highly accomplished students who had made it all the way to Johns Hopkins through diligence, devotion, and hard work; they would hardly throw it all away just to go crazy during a night on the town. No, this was going to turn out to be serious business.

He knocked on Chief Jeffrey Hubbins' door, heard the chief wrap up a call, and waited for the man to bid him entry. He did, and Torrey entered hesitantly. If he hadn't already heard about Jennifer Willis coming up missing, he would now, and it would likely prompt the leader to form some kind of a team. This made Torrey nervous because he had always preferred to work alone. Besides, he didn't think they should be jumping the gun; for all they knew the girls really were just letting off a little steam.

"Chief, how's your morning?" Torrey offered the man a pleasant smile, which Hubbins saw right through.

Hubbins leaned back in his chair and wove his fingers together, studying Torrey closely. "Your greeting tells me that yours isn't going so well. What have you got?"

"May I sit?"

Hubbins nodded toward the chair before his desk. "Please, do."

As Torrey lowered his body into the chair, he began to shuffle the papers around in his hands nervously. Hubbins waited patiently, and that was enough to tell Torrey that the man already had some level of "heads-up" on the cases. That was a bad sign, as far as workloads went.

"I got a call a few minutes ago from a Bradford Willis; his daughter is a genetics student here. It seems she hasn't answered her mother's calls for almost two days now, and they never miss calls... twice a day is the norm."

Hubbins continued to study him. "And I take it you don't suspect an overdue partier?"

"Well, sir, I would," Torrey continued. "But we also have the issue of the missing Sarah Russell, who has been missing for one week before the Willis girl. And neither of them have any kind of history for partying or skipping out in any manner. As a matter of fact, a quick computer check told me that neither girl has missed a class this year at all; this causes me to think that somehow the cases are related if you know what I mean."

"Show me the file."

Torrey handed the file over the desk to his superior, who proceeded to take the next ten minutes studying it. He nodded now and then, but mostly the chief shook his head. Torrey could tell that Chief Hubbins wasn't feeling any better about the whole thing than he was.

After a sufficient amount of time had passed, Torrey asked, "Are you going to want to form a team, or call off-campus cops in on the action and let me go about my beat?"

Hubbins tossed the manila envelope onto the blotter on his desk and steepled his fingertips beneath his chin. "On the contrary, with these two girls being top-notch students, I'm inclined to call in a couple of city investigators, but I think that initially, it will be vital for you to work with them. After all, you have access to student files that they would only stumble through, and your help would be invaluable to them... at least, it would initially, don't you think?"

"I do."

Hubbins nodded. "So, you're willing to at least give them a kickstart? These girls need to be found right away. I don't care if they're puking in the bathroom at some boyfriend's house and crashing on his couch. The fact is, I doubt very highly that is the case in either situation, don't you?"

Torrey nodded slowly. "I would be inclined to agree."

"Tell me, John... in the past week have you noticed anyone out of place on campus? Anyone who might be suspicious enough to fit the bill of an... an abductor?"

Right off the top of his head, he couldn't recall anyone fitting that description, but something was nagging at the base of his brain, and he couldn't quite put his finger on it. Hadn't there been an odd someone? Hadn't he encountered someone who just... well, just shouldn't have been where he was? He had dealt with so many students in the last several days that he was having a very difficult time pulling the evasive thing to mind, but he knew it was there, buried in the dark recesses of his brain. He made a mental note to dedicate some serious attention to pulling up the elusive incident and seeing if it was at all pertinent to the two cases.

"Um, not right off hand, though I have come across

many suspicious idiots this last week." Torrey felt ashamed of his answer, and he changed the subject. "So, I figured that if you are going to call in a couple of city boys, I need to pull the girls' class schedules and get their personal study schedules from roommates and friends, if at all possible. We might be able to tie the two incidents together somehow."

"I agree. You go ahead and get started on that; take Nick Manning with you and pound some pavement after the two of you pull their class schedules. That will give us a bit of a head start for when the city boys arrive. Go ahead and get started; I don't want Baltimore PD thinking we're sitting on our asses over here, right?"

"Right."

With that, Torrey rose and left Hubbins' office, his stomach in knots. He tracked down Manning in the break room and relayed the chief's orders to him, and together they went to their desks and hit the computers. Getting the girls' schedules was first. They would confer, go over them with a fine-tooth comb, then proceed to hop in a squad car and go to the places the missing girls lived for their personal schedules. With any luck, the girls would be in their places of residence, safe and sound. They would be able to lecture each one and go about their business.

But what John Torrey didn't know at that time was that this wasn't about to be a simple case... no, this thing was about to surprise and frighten the entire city of Baltimore.

The cellar was unusually quiet.

It had been nearly two full days since Melvin had brought home "Candy" (Jennifer Willis). The petite, auburn-haired girl had little to say or try to communicate since her awakening the day before. She had some light in her eyes, but Melvin believed that the lack of any kind of human exchange was due to the fact that she was in a strange place, didn't recognize him at all, and was having a terrible time with any kind of recall that would cause her to register emotion. She stared straight ahead, her eyes shifting here and there every now and then, and she kept her body still, in a fetal position beneath her blanket. Melvin felt odd about her as if she perhaps wasn't meant to be one of his, and he felt this for several reasons. First, he had administered a responsible medium procedure to her, but she didn't seem to show any kind of response to post-surgical testing. Second, she had a slight fever, and this, of course, concerned him. He had given her aspirin as soon as she had been able, just a short time ago, but neither seemed to have any effect on the fever. In fact, it had gone up a degree-and-a-half... not good. Even Melvin, in his own illness-addled mind, knew that he had to get the fever down, but the fact was, he just wasn't properly equipped in this old cellar with what was needed to properly get the job done.

But he wasn't about to go to any hospital. He was going to either figure it out, or his little Candy was going to die; it was that simple. He didn't care how much he loved his dear pets, there was no way he would put himself, or the happiness and contentment of the other two at risk just because one didn't "take."

He stayed with her and soothed her now and then, trying to get her to take water or even a tiny amount of soft food, but to no avail. Melvin knew she wouldn't last long at that rate, and he sat in a chair in her cell, journaling the entire circumstance and planning what he would do with her when she was gone. The dominant thought in his mind during this time was "Grateful for the crematory"; he would be fine.

But before that, he would have his way with her... yes, dead or alive. He didn't go through all the trouble of taking her just to get nothing but trouble out of it. Besides, the idea of ravishing her dead body didn't repulse him in the slightest. As a matter of fact, it aroused him enough to begin to hope that she would soon die. He didn't really want to make it with a sick body, just a dead one.

So, he sat with her and journaled, then jumped up now and then to check on Mother and Princess, who were doing wonderfully. Princess had been exceptionally quiet so far that day, and while he felt a pinch of concern about it, he was so wrapped up in Candy that he couldn't maintain his focus on the issue. Regardless, something inside of him tried to flag him down and tell him something was off. But she was quiet and overly-cooperative, making him even think on more than one occasion that she was flirting with him with her eyes. This was odd, and he was guarding himself against it. On the other hand, maybe she had broken much faster than he ever could have hoped for. He felt much safer, for some reason, sitting with Candy and caring for her until she either pulled through or gave up the ghost, whichever came first.

It didn't take as long as he expected. Candy did nothing but lay in her vegged-out, catatonic state until slowly, but surely, her eyes began to flutter. A short time later she closed her eyes for good, and the only thing that ever came out of her mouth was her final breath. Melvin weighed out briefly whether he wanted to scrutinize and analyze why it had gone the way it had, but he quickly opted to simply move on. He wouldn't wonder why... rather, he would assume her immune system was too weak to handle the surgery and he would simply find the next one and try again. There was no understandable reason for her death; all he knew was that her last temperature he had taken on Candy had shown a fever of 104.8 degrees, so certainly it was a major contributor to her death.

But he had been unable to take his mind off of the sex he had been looking forward to. Now that she was dead, he could have his way with her, and he did. It was not all it had been cracked up to be. She was chilling as time passed, also taking away from the joy of the experience, not to mention that she gave him no response, which was simply not what he wanted or expected from his pets. Screaming or moaning, he wanted something, some kind of a response to whet his proverbial appetite.

He waited then until nearly two in the morning when he decided the time was right to light the crematory fire. He knew he should have been preparing for the ridding of the body. As her body burned in the messy crematory, he decided that from now on, he would dispose of the dead immediately.

Now, as he cleaned and sanitized her cell, he decided that it was time to get the next one, the one to take Candy's place. Then and only then would he take a break for a while. Certainly, the law was looking into two missing girls.

He would watch the news that night and find out before venturing out again for the next one.

R.W.K. Clark

CHAPTER 12

John Torrey sat in an on-campus conference room in the campus police station. He was in the company of Campus Officer Nicholas Manning, and they were joined by city police detectives Jimmy Cohen and Richie Miller from Missing Persons. The four men had been conducting interviews with Johns Hopkins students whom they had connected to either Sarah Russell or Jennifer Willis in some way, shape, or form. It was two in the afternoon, and so far that day they had completed almost fifteen interviews. All four men were exhausted, and there were really no leads in sight.

"I have to tell you, men, that I just don't think this was a job done by a fellow student." Lieutenant Cohen was seasoned at his job, and the tone of his voice was enough for Sergeant Torrey to believe him. They had endured tears on the part of the women interviewees, and anger on the part of the men. Not one of the people they had spoken to had struck any of the men as suspects at all. As a matter of fact, with each passing interview, all four men had felt more and more like they were wasting their time. "To me, my gut feeling says this was an outside job all the way."

Torrey nodded and sighed as he sat back in his chair and laced his fingers behind his head. "I tend to agree. I have three more people on the list for today; lets at least see what they have to say, then we can determine what we are going to move forward with tomorrow. I have to tell you, though, I'm ready to start pounding the pavement."

With all of them in agreement, the next person was brought in. Janelle Hanson happened to be a close friend of Jennifer Willis'. In fact, she was one of the friends that Willis intended to meet for a late supper, drinks, and dancing at a club near her dorm. The girl walked into the conference room with red-rimmed eyes and several wadded up tissues clutched tightly in her right hand. Her left hand gripped the double-handles of an expensive Coach bag that Torrey could recognize as the real deal; he had to deal with a ring of crooks selling knock-offs on campus about eighteen months prior, and he had gained a fairly good education on women's accessories in the process.

Janelle sat while Nick Manning fetched her a styrofoam cup of water. The interview began with basic questions on the part of the city boys, with Torrey jumping in with his own only now and again. The girl really knew nothing; she had been waiting for her friend to arrive that night, along with her boyfriend and another young man who was to be a blind date to Miss Willis. According to the young woman, Jennifer was never late; she actually was obsessive about being on time. When only five minutes had passed after she was due to arrive, Janelle had started to feel concerned. There was no reason for the girl to be late, Janelle insisted, both to her friends that night and to police right then. She was walking a mere two blocks; she had a cell, and she would have called if held up for any reason. By the time fifteen minutes had passed, both Janelle and her boyfriend had started to call the girl's cell, thinking that maybe she had chickened out about the whole "blind date" gig, even though that wasn't like her at all. They had been startled to discover that the phone went right to voicemail. An hour later, they were banging on the door of her dorm room and being told by her roommate that she had left at the exact time she should have. The roommate convinced them to not panic, claiming that Jennifer may have run into her ex, and the two were likely reconciling as they spoke. But Janelle hadn't slept the entire night worrying about her friend. Even so, she had gone ahead and pushed it out of her mind and managed to enjoy the remainder of her weekend, ignoring the nagging concern in her brain and stomach. Jennifer was a grown woman, after all, and accomplished at that. It was almost insulting for her to worry, she had concluded.

Jennifer's parents had contacted campus police two mornings after the blind date was to take place, concerned about the two missed calls her mother had made.

Their next interview was with a kid who studied with Sarah Russell at the Eisenhower Library on a regular basis. They had two courses together, and they split the studies on them over three nights per week; the pair, apparently, knew each other fairly well.

His name was Brian Kimball, and he seemed to be sick with worry over his study partner. Brian would have been a suspect, but for the fact that on the night she came up missing, he was with his girlfriend, who was not a Johns Hopkins student. The pair lived together, and she worked at a high-end restaurant off-campus that dealt out very demanding hours. When she had time off, she spent it with Brian, and that happened to be the first night in a month she actually had an evening to enjoy her personal life. Police had spoken with the girlfriend and were satisfied. Now they just wanted to ask Brian if Sarah had complained of anyone harassing her or stalking her; Brian insisted that she had not. Everything had been normal with Sarah on the last night they had studied together, which was the night before she had disappeared. The interview was brief, and Brian Kimball left the conference room with a downcast face and a very morose disposition.

Finally, the last person they interviewed for the day entered and sat down. The young man was a first-year student at Johns Hopkins, but he knew Sarah through mutual friends and from attending parties and clubs they both happened to frequent. It was as simple as them both running with the same crowd. As it turned out, Sarah, for all her high grades, responsibility, and ambition, enjoyed cutting loose quite often. Because of this, she likely didn't put up her guard around strangers as she should have.

His name was Jerry Collins, and he drove a dark green truck with gold accents. The truck made him stand out, and as it happened, another student had observed Jerry at a stop light ogling Sarah the day before her disappearance. This had been one of several reasons he had been called in for an interview. But after questioning the young man about the exchange, police were convinced it was innocent enough.

But then Jerry told them about the van that had been sitting next to him.

According to him, there had been a man in an old white cargo van. He, too, had noticed the cute Sarah, and according to Jerry, he had caught her eye and even gotten a smile out of her; why, Jerry didn't know. He had been surprised at the smile himself because the guy at the wheel had been something of a "creepy-looking dude," not the type of guy that Sarah would have given attention to at all. To Jerry, it had seemed like she was either in an exceptionally bouncy mood, or she was flirting intentionally, strictly for the fun of it.

But that hadn't been what made the incident stick in his mind; none of that had done it. What had done it was the fact that the guy in the van had pulled through the light and flipped the van around and followed her. Jerry had caught it all in his rearview mirror, and while it had concerned him slightly, he had brushed it off by telling himself that the guy knew her, and that was why she had returned his grin.

The four cops asked Jerry a few more questions, mostly about the van and the guy inside, before excusing him and thanking him for his time. They made sure he had a business card from one of the city boys in case he remembered anything more, then he rose to leave.

Cohen stopped him. "Say, Jerry, what time of day was this incident?"

Jerry shrugged. "Early evening, around six-thirty or seven, I was on my way to see a girl I have been trying to get to know. Yeah, that's about right."

It had happened the night before she disappeared, and from the description of the incident and the scene at which it took place, it was obvious to all four cops that Sarah had been on her way to meet Brian at the Eisenhower Library. The guy must have followed her there.

Something began to spark in Torrey's mind then, as they discussed the information Jerry Collins had given them, but it kept slipping from his grasp. He was tired, and as the other three talked and took notes, he tried to retrieve whatever information was bothering him, but to no avail. He didn't want to mention it to the others until he brought it to mind, so he made a bold note on his pad and joined the conversation. He would review the info when he got home, and he would do it over and over until it came to him.

But for now the men were done, and happy to be. They broke up the meeting, agreed to reconvene in the same place at eight the following morning, and said their goodnights. All of them wanted to go home and get some rest, and all of them were hoping against hope that another girl wouldn't come up missing in the meantime.

That same evening, Melvin was busying himself with the bathing, feeding, and tucking in of his pets. He wanted to get them settled in early because he planned to hit the streets in search of his next success story as soon as possible. He didn't plan to hit the campus again; he had watched the news and now knew that was the worst idea possible.

No, he planned to hit a small apartment complex about three blocks off campus, but on the side of the campus that was nowhere near where he found the first two stray pets. That way it would be city police involved, and it would take a bit more time for them to connect the dots if he was careful. But Melvin knew that the city police picking up the scent also meant that if he kept things up locally, the FBI would get involved much sooner. Even he knew that when things like this were clumped together in one area, the FBI came to notice; that wouldn't do at all.

So, he did what he had to do at home and set his sights on heading to the apartment complex. He doubted he would get lucky right away for the third time in a row, but he had to start somewhere, and that place seemed as good as any, as it would keep him off the campus and away from campus police's prying eyes. He would be surprised if that cop he met outside Eisenhower Library hadn't thought of coming across him sleeping in the van; that had been stupid and irresponsible. A strange dude that wasn't a student sleeping in a van for no apparent reason. Well, the cops hadn't come to the door yet, and that was all he was worried about. For now, he had priorities, and worrying wasn't one of them.

He did a quick walk-through of the cellar, taking special time at the door of each cell to gaze in on his two lovelies. While he stood at Princess' door, he thought he might have a bit of fun with her when the next procedure was complete, and the pet was recovering. Yes, he had some pretty cool ideas already building up in his head. They would have to go if he was going to do the evening's work right.

Within the hour he was pulling out of the main gate of the property. He was driving a dark blue station wagon if that was what you would call the sporty looking vehicle. It had been one his mother purchased several years back for the novelty of owning it. Perhaps she had driven it once before moving onto an SUV that was yellow. Anyway, she had made sure it was maintained, like the other vehicles she owned, but she never gave the car a second glance. With all of that being said, Melvin thought it wise to eliminate the use of the van for the time being and put one of her other toys to use. He had always wanted to drive the car, and now he was.

It was a beautiful night; the sky was clear and starry, and the wind was mild and warm. Melvin thought it was a perfect night to complete his mission, and he had even dressed for the weather. He donned khaki cargo shorts and a cream colored t-shirt with a band's logo on it, and he had decided to eliminate the glasses in exchange for contacts. He had found a brand new pair from before his accident, and though they were an outdated prescription, Melvin could see clearly enough to get away with wearing them. He felt that the entire "get up," as his mother would have called his wardrobe choice, would lessen any anxiety his potential pet might feel upon encountering him. To be honest, he looked and felt more like a student of Johns Hopkins than he had before he took that knock to his head.

So, he was off and running. He had music playing in his car, and he had the windows down so he could enjoy the night air. As he tapped his fingers on the steering wheel to the beat of each song, he directed the vehicle toward the apartment complex he had in mind, situated only two or three blocks southwest of the actual Johns Hopkins campus. His mood was very light; at least, it was until he rounded the last corner to the apartments. That was when he stopped the car in its tracks.

The apartments were gone; there was nothing but an empty field with tall, blowing grass.

Melvin sat there, right in the middle of the road, and stared at the field in disbelief. In his mind's eye, he had been able to clearly picture the entire place, even its parking lot. He had an acquaintance who had lived there when he was still a student at the university. They had studied together for Advanced Child Psych on several occasions. Now the place was just... gone. A memory.

It took several moments and a car horn from behind him to jolt Melvin back to reality. As he pulled over to the curb so the car behind him could pass, he remembered why he was even there. He couldn't let something like this get to him... why was it bothering him so much, anyway? He realized, almost immediately, that it was because he had missed so much life while in his coma; he almost had no idea where he was, or even who he was. Had their study sessions ever really been? Or had it all been just a figment of his imagination, a trumped-up past that never really existed?

Melvin sat there for the next ten minutes, even though he was fully aware that time was ticking away. It was the first real reality check he had since coming out of his coma, thanks to sweet Adele. He needed to process the fact that, for a moment, he felt as though he might not be in his right mind.

Of course, he was... of course. This was just a minor shock to the system, a spooking of his mentality that was all. Melvin began to forcefully shake it off, determined to rid himself of the lost and overwhelmed feelings the sight of the empty field had caused. It was time to get his bearings and get back down to business.

So, here he was, in the perfect neighborhood, anyway. He cleared his mind and began to get a good look around him. There were several houses located across both cross-streets of the corner where the apartments had been. Most all of them were illuminated, most even giving off the bluish flicker of television screens dancing from within. On the left side of the street, about a block and a half up, Melvin could see a young couple walking slowly; they paused just under a streetlight and kissed before continuing on.

Clear on the other side of the field, which was around three acres total, he could see the lights of a tavern. A neon beer sign skipped a beat every three seconds or so, going totally black. But from where he sat, Melvin could see people going in and coming out of the establishment. Suddenly, for the first time in years, an ice-cold beer sounded very, very good to him, especially because drinking was something only his mother saw fit to do. Others who drank liquor or beer were no more than vagrants who didn't know their asses from a hole in the ground when it came to life and living it.

Yes, a cold beer was almost necessary.

Melvin pulled away from the curb and turned the car's nose in the direction of the tavern. As he approached, he saw several more people, both entering and exiting. From where he had sat on the other side of the lot, it had looked like the place was small, and therefore, quite crowded inside. Now, as he neared the establishment, he realized that it was much bigger than it had at first appeared. It was long, and the rear part of the building was out of view where he had been. Yes, there were likely a few prospects inside that he could take under serious consideration.

He pulled into a lot behind the building that was obviously too small to accommodate the number of people who were actually frequenting the place; there wasn't an empty spot for him at all, which he found more than annoying. He pulled out of the lot on the other side, driving right over the curb, then rounded the block. After several minutes of rubbernecking back and forth, Melvin spotted an empty gap outside of a deserted-looking home about four doors down, behind the bar. He parallel parked, then sat there a moment staring at the place. He had never in his entire life been in a place like this; how did one act? Was there a particular persona one was to acquire if they were to frequent such a place? He wasn't sure, but in the end, Melvin came to a conclusion that, as he was told in kindergarten, it was best to be oneself, no matter what.

He looked into the rearview mirror and ran his fingers through his hair. He found himself wondering why he didn't sport contact lenses more often; he certainly was more attractive when he wore them than when he donned his black-framed specs. With a small burst of energy, Melvin realized that he looked just like everyone else he had seen enter the tavern, and his apprehension left him in a whoosh of air. This, along with a couple of cold ones, was going to be a breeze.

He opened the driver's door to the car, then paused and sat back to reinsert the ignition key and roll up the windows. Melvin didn't think that it would be a good idea to lock the doors, just in case his next pet came slinking along, and he even made sure that the rear tailgate was unlocked, so putting her inside would be easy. But rolling up the windows seemed to be paramount, considering any passerby may view the sedan as fair game.

Finally, Melvin was able to step out into the night.

He took a deep, nervous breath, putting the car keys in his right front pocket as he did so. He tried to pry his mind off his quest and focus on the cold beverages he would find inside; perhaps if he changed his focus, he would be able to literally notice a true easy mark if it looked him in the eye. Maybe not, but he was counting on it.

Slowly, and with a bit of shyness encompassing his being, Melvin started toward the main entrance. For the first time, he noticed a dying neon sign above the door that read "The Thirsty Irishman." It buzzed and flickered annoyingly, touching the itch in his brain that never seemed to completely go away. He ignored it, and pushed open the double-paned glass door and went from the darkness to only one step above.

The room was abuzz with music and conversation. In the far right corner, a pair of hoodlum-looking young men with ponytails and beautiful girlfriends were playing a game of pool; on the right, a couple of clean-cut men who were apparently going solo shooting a game of darts. Behind the bar stood a young man with a bunch of peach fuzz on his chin; he was mixing a concoction suited for a die-hard alcoholic only. A raggedy looking female of about twenty-five or twenty-six poured a beer for worn out biker-types; the two were obviously flirting, and it made him feel uncomfortable from clear across the room.

He couldn't let these people throw him off; Melvin toughened his demeanor and made his way to an empty stool that sat at the half-circle-shaped bar. Sitting down, he smiled at an older woman next to him. She smiled back and turned her full attention to his presence.

"Wouldn't wanna buy an old broad a sip, would ya?" she asked.

Melvin smiled at her; she was by no means his type, but it wasn't above him to accommodate a lady, especially one who wouldn't be able to find another buyer for days if she was lucky.

"Sure thing," he replied. "What are you drinking?"

The woman ordered a rum and cola, and he put in the order, including a cold beer for himself in a frosty mug. While they waited, Melvin let his eyes wander around the room so he could get a better look at what was going on around him. At the end of the bar were two girls who could have been sexy, young college students, but they were obviously on their second or third hour of drinking, and that simply wouldn't do. Or maybe it would...

The drinks came, and Melvin offered his neighbor her beverage with a smile, bidding her well in enjoying the liquor to its completion. He, however, decided to pick up his beer and make his way to the two girls who, at this point, were both leaning slightly to the left. He took the stool next to the one who wasn't sitting against the wall, supporting her head with the hard, finished oak.

He sat down and made himself comfortable, taking a long, drawn-out drink from his beer.

"Hey," he opened, "how's it going tonight?"

The girl was slender, with tanned skin and dark

circles of exhaustion under her eyes. She had long brown hair that spilled down her back, and green eyes which almost sparkled. Melvin quickly determined that these were her two best traits.

"Hey," she replied, her voice bored and unenthusiastic.

He took another long draw and turned back to her. "For as many people as I see here, this place is all but dead."

She snorted. "Yeah, it always is, but it's walking distance from home."

He laughed. "That's important, alright."

The girl began to study him while her female companion began to snore. "You look familiar... you come here often?"

Melvin recognized the old, worn-out line, but it didn't bother him in the slightest. "No, actually. This is my first time. I'm from the other side of town, on the other side of the Hopkins. Most of our bars are a bit more... I don't know... proper, as my uptight mother would put it. I personally hate the way the rich judge the poor; I'd much rather hang out in a laid back place like this."

The pair sat in silence, but he knew that she was pondering what he had said, and he considered that as him being a step ahead. He purposefully averted his eyes from her, but she had no idea that he was clearly watching her from the corners of them.

Melvin knew that she was buying his lines. It didn't even matter if he was able to get her into the sedan or not that night; all that mattered to him was that she had more trust in him when he left than when he walked in the flea-bitten joint. It seemed to him that was precisely what was happening.

"So," she began, seemingly coming out of nowhere with the statement, "Do you live around here? I mean, close by?"

He gave her something of a sideways smile, took a sip of his beer, and nodded. "Not too far, anyway. About ten minutes."

"I just live up the block," she said in a low voice, her eyes shifting around the room as if to look for unsavory types that may have heard her. "This is my friend, Melinda. She's something of a lightweight, but I bring her because it's unsafe to go out alone these days."

"I'd have to say I agree," he whispered, leaning over to make sure she heard. "You never know who you will run into."

Melvin picked up his beer and slammed it, then nodded at the female bartender to let her know he wanted another. When he was sure she was fetching it for him, he turned back to the girl. She was holding up her head with her hand and staring at her mostly-gone pink drink.

"Can I buy you another?" he asked.

She studied him out of the corner of her eye. "I don't make it a practice to let strangers buy drinks for me."

Melvin smiled. "Okay, then. I'm Mel. What's your name?"

"Denise," she said slowly. "Denise Hoskins."

"Well, Denise, it looks like we are just about the two loneliest people in this place." He took another drink of his beer and gazed around nonchalantly as if looking for someone else who just may fall into the category with them.

She chuckled. "I'd have to agree with you, especially since Miss Party Pooper over here can't seem to find anything to smile about."

Melvin looked over Denise's companion much more closely. She was a bit chubby, with greasy-looking black hair and too much eyeliner, which appeared to be running down her cheeks as she slept. Out of the left corner of her mouth, a stringer of drool was making its way to the surface of the bar. Melvin grabbed a napkin and placed it beneath her face to catch the impending pool of saliva.

Denise smiled. "That was nice. What do you say we get out of here, just you and me? We could go to my place; I mean, I room with Sleepy here, but she'll be fine. She dates one of the guys at the dartboard; all I'd have to do was tell him that I was leaving, and he'd make sure she'd get home safely."

Melvin glanced over his shoulder at the two guys shooting darts; he really didn't want to be confronted by either of them, because they both looked a bit too buff for his taste. Maybe this entire bar thing wasn't a good idea. Besides, he was starting to get a buzz so he wouldn't be on top of his game no matter what. The last thing he needed was to cause some kind of a scene because he wasn't cautious enough in who he chose for his next pet. This barfly was likely not even worth it at all.

Denise must have sensed his apprehension, and she put her hand on his arm to get his attention. "Don't worry about the guys. Benny could really care less about Drowsy over here. He's just known her and her family for so long that he would feel obligated."

Melvin smiled. "I don't know about going to your house... after all, you are a stranger and everything." He noticed immediately that his words of reassurance had worked... either that, or the beer was really taking away his inhibitions, and his ability to make good judgment calls. "Maybe my place is better. After all, I live in a pretty big house, and we could party undisturbed all night long."

"You have anything good?" Denise asked, her once red and tired eyes suddenly perking up. "I mean, I would really love to hop on a cloud right about now."

He wanted to vomit in her face, but he forced his smile to grow. "Denise, there are more than enough clouds to go around at my place."

Without further hesitation, the girl jumped up and made her way over to the dart shooters. Melvin watched her and took note of her figure: not bad. She is a cute little package that fills out her jeans nicely, with boobs that jiggled when she walks, and a head of thick, full hair that he hadn't noticed when she was holding up her head with her hand. Yes, she would do quite nicely, barfly druggie or not.

She grabbed the guy in the blue shirt by the arm, and he leaned over to listen to what she was saying in his ear. He glanced over at Sleeping Beauty, barely giving Melvin a second glance, said something in return to her and then turned back to his game. Denise made her way over to Melvin with a broad smile on her face. She grabbed her purse off the bar and whispered in his ear, "All set."

As the two left the bar, Melvin was in shock. This was so easy, much easier than the first two. Hell, he wouldn't even have to use any of his chloroform on this one, and he was all about conserving.

Soon, the pair was tooling down the road in the sedan, past the barren field that used to be filled with apartments, and toward his home near Johns Hopkins. Melvin listened to Denise raving about what a cool car he had, and how cute he was, and how their meeting must have been meant to be because she was half in love with him already.

Melvin was in love too... so in love that he was taking her home for keeps. He would take her away from the dreary world he had just found her in and introduce her to complete contentment and freedom once and for all. He would show her that he could truly provide and care for those he was responsible for. And he would show her how to truly have fun, fun that didn't involve catatonic friends, bars, and loneliness that seemed to last forever.

CHAPTER 13

"Wow, Mel... this is like some kind of mansion or something."

Denise was enthralled with all things "Ken." He had to remind her of his name more than once on the way to his house, which told him she was way more messed up than he had initially thought, and this pleased him. Her level of intoxication would deepen the effects of her pills he planned to give her... in small doses, of course. It wouldn't do for her to die right there without him even getting another go around at the procedure that had failed so miserably the last time. He was sure that he had the right amount calculated for his desires with Candy, but she just hadn't taken to the procedure at all. It had been a disappointment, but Denise here was his chance to prove it again.

"I guess you could say that. I grew up in places like this, so they really don't phase me anymore."

Denise stood in the main foyer, which was really the size of a small bowling alley, and began to spin around, dancing with enthralled excitement. "It's beautiful... just beautiful. A girl like me would feel like a queen living this way."

Her happy demeanor was making Melvin
uncomfortable, and feeling uncomfortable tended to
make him a bit angry these days. "Listen, let's go to the
library and get a drink; what do you say?"

She stopped her twirling around and looked at him,
smiling broadly. "Library? Like with books?"

"Is there any other kind?" Melvin tried to smile
back, but it didn't touch his eyes.

She began to follow him as he walked. "I suppose
not. I love books; reading is probably one of my
favorite things to do."

He reached out and turned the ornate brass knob on
the library door. "After partying and hanging out at
bars, I suppose?"

Denise stopped and stared at him as he reached
inside the library door and turned on the light. "Um, are
you alright, Mel? I didn't say something that pissed you
off, did I?"

He realized that his attitude had changed, and he
suddenly became concerned that he was scaring her off.
That was the last thing he wanted. After all, he had
brought her here to become a permanent member of his
little family. It was best to feign cheer, even though she
had annoyed him with her love for the house. Just
because he saw his place as something of a prison didn't
mean that a girl like her would. In all likelihood, she saw
it as a castle... maybe she even saw him as a prince. It
would be best if he acts like one now.

"Nah," he said, following it with a chuckle. "I guess
I'm just used to a place like this, and it seems that all my

life people shied away from me because of... because of the money and all."

She relaxed a bit, and they both stepped inside the library. While he mixed a couple of drinks, spiking hers with a bit of pills, she wandered around looking at the books, caressing their spines as if they were old lovers. He watched her out of the corner of his eye, slightly amused by the change in her personality from the bar to now.

He finished the drinks and turned around with both of them in his hands. He had whipped her up a pinkish concoction with a bit of grenadine and an ample dose of pills; he had a small whiskey sour. He didn't want to lose control; it was important that once he had her incapacitated and ready for the procedure that he was on top of his game. Melvin watched her for a moment longer then interrupted her reverie.

"Here's your drink," he said pleasantly. "Make yourself comfortable, Denise. You have plenty of time to look at the books."

She walked over to him and took the beverage, then sipped it before taking a big gulp. "Yum. Fruity." She sat down on the leather sofa and got comfortable while Melvin put Boston on the stereo.

"So, tell me, do you like morphine?"

Denise smiled at him over the rim of her glass, which was already half gone, and answered him in a slightly slurred voice. "I don't shoot up; I'm not a junkie. But if you have a pill or two, I would love it."

He stepped into the small bathroom off the library,

where he was now keeping some of Mother's medication. Fishing two small pills out of the bottle, he returned to her and handed them over. Denise wasted no time in downing them. Melvin sat down on the far end of the couch, opposite her.

"Do you like science?" he asked.

Denise shrugged and drained her drink. "Sure, I suppose. I mostly like that it's dependable, unlike the rest of the world. I got good marks in school in it, but unfortunately, my family wasn't the type to really put a high priority on education." Her voice turned sad. "I could've been so much more... so much more."

She was getting drowsy now. Melvin had initially planned to show her the basement, but now it looked like she was going to pass right out on him. That was better; he could get going with his plans without any kind of fight. So, he began to drone on boringly about psychiatry and lobotomies and the like, and it didn't take long for the girl to begin to lightly snore. He rose and took the glass from her hand and set it on the end table. Then he stood and looked at her for a long time. She was much prettier than he had initially thought, though life showed on her face. That was fine; he would take great joy in making her the best she could be. He hoped the others would like her; he had a feeling they would.

Soon, Melvin picked her up from the sofa as a mother would a baby and slowly, limping, carried her to the cellar stairs. He made sure to enter the area as quietly as possible, so as not to wake the others, then he took her to her cell; she would have the one on the end on the right, directly across from Princess. After checking on Mother and Princess, he strapped Denise to her gurney, turned the radio on low, and got to work.

He had a good feeling about this one, he thought as he undressed her and looked her body over. With the right calculation, he might be able to pull her through enough to actually converse with him on a limited basis. After all, she loved books, and so did he. He would have to make sure she had a good selection to read, once she was able of course.

Before long she was completely under sedation, and Melvin had shaved her head in the front and began the drilling. Neither Princess nor Mother stirred, as he had dosed them well before putting them down. He would be busy for the next couple of hours, after all, and couldn't afford to tend to them with such an important task at hand.

With a smile on his face, he proceeded.

∞

Torrey, Manning, and city boys Lieutenant Cohen and Detective Miller were all back in the campus conference room the following morning, a new stack of manila envelopes in front of them, each detailing the day's interviews. There was only ten total, and while they were beginning to see an end in sight regarding the interview process, none of them had much hope for any new leads.

Torrey had fretted all night over the spark that Jerry Collins' interview had caused in his mind. It was something about a white cargo van, and he knew that he had recently seen one, even spoke to the driver. But campus cops were constantly dealing with students, so much in fact, that he wouldn't doubt it if he was just confused. He couldn't seem to drag his mind away, however, but by the time the first interviewee, a girl coincidentally named Jennifer, like one of the victims, arrived, he forced the thoughts away; it was time to focus. Jennifer Tiller was in her final year at the college, and she had been very good friends with Jennifer Willis, even living on the same floor in the same dorm. They had called her in because they had found out that Miss Willis had invited her to go along with her on the blind date, just to alleviate tension and have a little fun with her own boyfriend in the meantime. They were to meet at the end of the dorm lot, but Willis had never shown up.

Tiller was a beautiful girl. She was studying psychiatry for juvenile delinquents on drugs and specializing in dealing with the after-effects of drug use on the juvenile brain, and how to properly treat it. She entered the room with a sad countenance, but with confidence, ready and willing to give them all the information she had.

The officers began questioning by asking about the history of the two friends, discussing any enemies that Willis may have had, and finally asking about the details of the night in question. Jennifer began to speak, and loads of information came out. She even mentioned that the only drawback of dating for her friend Willis was the fact that her prior boyfriend; she had become apprehensive about things after that, just wanting to go slow.

But then Tiller mentioned how she understood. She talked about a small intellectual crush she had on a student a few years back; he had been interested in more, of course, but outside of his intellect, she had not. She mentioned how she had seen him at the bus stop one day, and then he suffered a terrible accident and was in a coma for an extended time. She had tried to visit him shortly after he woke, but he hadn't been the same, and his mother had put a kibosh on the visit.

His name had been Melvin; she couldn't recall his last name, except to say that it reminded her of what you would call someone who was a tattle-tale, or a snitch. It was obvious that the girl was trying to wrack her brain, but she was becoming more and more frustrated with herself.

Torrey, on the other hand, was practically on the edge of his seat. He had just spoken to that guy... Melvin what's-his-name... only a couple of weeks before. He had been sleeping in a white cargo van outside of Eisenhower Library, and if Torrey remembered correctly, it had been the night before Sarah Russell had gone missing. Had he been there, stalking her and waiting for her to come out?

"Fink!" Jennifer suddenly shouted with a smile. "No, that's not it... Frink that was it. Calvin Frink!"

"Melvin," Torrey said his mind racing. "His name is Melvin Frink, and he had been a neuro-psych major before his accident. Um, embarrassingly enough, I just recently encountered him on campus under somewhat unusual circumstances."

Manning, Cohen, and Miller, as well as Jennifer Tiller, all looked at him, their mouths open slightly, their eyes full of expectation. Torrey just sighed and sat back in his chair, then ran his fingers through what was left of the hair on top of his head.

"I want to start off by saying that after we interviewed Jerry Collins yesterday, something had been nagging at me, though I couldn't put a finger on it. I lost sleep last night trying to figure it out. Thanks to Jennifer here, I remember." Torrey paused and made eye contact with each of them. "I think it would be appropriate for Miss Tiller here to be excused before we go on, gentlemen."

The men all agreed, thanked Jennifer for her help, and graciously side-stepped her prying questions as they practically pushed her out the door. When they were all seated once again, all eyes were back on Torrey, who was sitting there looking not only sheepish but sick as well.

"It was the night before the Russell girl disappeared, the night that Jerry Collins said he saw a white van next to him at the stop light that turned around and followed her. Anyway, I was on patrol in the Eisenhower Library district, and it was getting late. I happened to be scouting the library parking lot, and the darker it got, the more cars left. But there was this van that was there for a fairly extensive amount of time. I kept my eye on it, and kept up my stroll, watching students come out of

Eisenhower, and either walk away or get into their vehicles and leave. Well, the lot was thinning out pretty good, and soon it was dark, the lot lights were on, and there were only a handful of cars left, mostly staff members; but the van was still there, so I went over to check it out.

"This guy was sitting in the van, fast asleep. I knocked on the window a few times... it took me a bit to wake him. But soon he woke, rolled down the window, and gave me his name. He told me he had been a student and was just reminiscing over old times. He said he had a bad accident a few years back and could no longer attend; he also said that was the reason he was sleeping... he got tired real easy, or something like that. I remembered his accident; it had been fairly big news. He got hit in the head by a falling beam at a construction site... ruined his entire future. He was one of the well-to-doers here in town... lived with his mother still in some mansion in Guilford, both while he was in attendance, and to this day, according to him. Anyway, he was friendly, not suspicious in the least, and since I remembered the accident and all, I advised him that the campus wasn't the best place to hang out these days, not like before. I told him there were lots of lowlifes, and that crime had risen, and I asked him to head home. He did, without incident."

Both of the city cops were jotting furiously in their tablets while Manning drew a stick figure in his and appeared to be pondering what Torrey had just revealed. The room was silent for several minutes, then

Cohen finally spoke up.

"Sounds like we have a suspect, alright."

Manning stopped doodling. "So, should we track down an address for the dude and pay him a visit?"

"I would vote to hold off," Miller stated matter-of-factly. "We need to get a history on this guy. You know, find out about past crimes if there are any, look into family history and mental conditions, especially if he suffered a brain injury. We all well know what one can do to the human personality. I mean, he may have been as gentle as a lamb before, but now... who knows?"

Torrey turned to Nick Manning. "Go see what you can find on Melvin Frink, or any Frink in the area, for that matter. And don't come back here with nothing, because we know he has a history here, criminal or not. I'm gonna get on my phone and see what the internet can give me."

Manning jumped up and left the office with a curt nod while Torrey got on his phone, as did Miller. Lieutenant Cohen pulled his laptop out of the case on the floor next to his chair and got the Wi-Fi password for the campus police station from Torrey before going on his own search.

∞

Twenty minutes later, Manning returned with a thin manila file folder. "What did you guys find?" he asked.

"Not a thing," Cohen replied with disgust. "Just a bunch of newspaper articles on his accident, a couple of articles giving him acclaim when he attended here for his work, some mentions of his mother Adele for local charitable contributions, and an obit on his father from Boston. I assume he and his mother moved here to Baltimore once the man died."

"Now, how about you?"

Manning tossed the file folder on the table with disgust, then crossed his arms over his chest. "Not a thing. Just copies of the city police reports from when the guy got knocked in the head, and a couple of ambulance reports verifying that the police released the patient from the scene and the treatment that was done on site, before transport."

"What hospital was he taken to?" Miller asked.

Manning snorted as he sat forward and flipped open the file. "Meadows Community, as per usual. He was under the care of a Dr. Fitzsimmons, a medical doctor specializing in neurology and brain and spinal injuries. The file also lists a psych doctor by the name of Philip Arondale, but I'm not sure how he's involved; it was a physical injury. All it says is that he was contacted by EMTs at the insistence of his mother, who showed up on site within minutes of police calling her."

"Where did the accident happen again?" This came from Nick Manning.

Torrey sat forward. "Well, you've got the address right there, but for the sake of detail, it took place where the new commerce building is now, on Calvert, by the main bus exchange. It's not too far from Guilford, where his address is listed as being. The truth is, my memory may be foggy, but it seemed to me that Frink always rode a bike... he never drove. He was sort of a nerdy fellow, at least by appearances. I mean, I can recollect him wearing a helmet sometimes, but that was mostly on rainy days, and he always wore a suit and tie when he was on campus."

"Preparing for the professional world," Cohen mumbled, more to himself than to the others. "Okay, listen, we need to work as a team on this all the way, because we don't even know if the missing girls were even taken off the campus at all, and if they weren't, well, me and Miller are out of our jurisdiction... at least until a crime is proven. With that being said, the two of us will pay a visit to this Dr. Fitzsimmons at Meadows Community Hospital; they'll be more open to city police than campus cops... no offense. Torrey, you and your sidekick, should stay here and make a few calls. For instance, get ahold of this psychiatrist Philip Arondale. Maybe he can shed some light on the character of Frink since his accident. And give Adele Frink a call as well. I don't want to spook the guy, see, in case he is our man, so when you talk to the mother make like you have some possessions that were found of his that you would like to return. Maybe even tell her the two of you were pals of sorts, and you'd like to visit to see how he's doing."

"Got it."

With that, all four men stood up and began to gather their things. Torrey planned to put Manning onto Adele Frink; the kid had dealt with a lot of parents since he'd been on staff, and he was especially good with the mothers. Torrey would handle calling Arondale; he had a bit of a background in psychiatry thanks to his father being a shrink. He felt like he would have a better understanding of what the guy might have to say than the kid would.

As they left the conference room, Torrey hoped against hope that this didn't turn out to be a dead-end lead. He had a sinking feeling in his gut that this wasn't the end of the abductions, and he wanted to put a stop to them before campus-wide panic broke out. The only way to keep the students safe was to keep them as calm as possible.

CHAPTER 14

Melvin pounded away at his newest pet, his eyes fixed on the rope burns on her wrists, though he had shut out her muffled cries. Denise, whom he had renamed "Green Eyes," had come through the procedure beautifully. She could even mumble some words, and he knew that the calculation was right at last. The first words she had said to him, though garbled and spit-filled, had been unintelligible.

She was a fighter, and when he had first tried to take her, she had nearly broken his nose. Melvin had ended up giving her pills to mellow her out so he could tie her up. Now she was splayed out in the middle of her cell on her mat, spread-eagled, with her arms tied tightly; her wrists were bleeding, as were her ankles, which were bound with the same kind of rope around a pair of posts that had served as lighting units years ago.

He had a cushion under her, holding her rear up in the air, and he had ahold of her hair like it was the reins of a horse. As he penetrated her, he cursed at her and slammed her head against the mat without realizing it. Small trickles of blood were coming out from under the bandage that covered the hole on the left side of her forehead. She was gagged with a clean wadded up sock, and the tape was wrapped around her head and neck to hold it in place. From Princess' cell, he could almost hear faint crying, but he didn't care. His mother, on the other hand, was emulating the grunting and groaning noises that he was making, taking breaks only to cackle loudly now and then. But Green Eyes' fighting, Princess' sobs, and Mother's aping served only to turn him on more. It made it more intimate, like family incest, if you will.

As a matter of fact, Melvin had been entertaining the thought of bringing Mother in on the action. After all, she seemed so gung-ho when he was going at it with one of his other girls. Pictures of his mother lying beneath him, cackling and grunting, her hacked up brain giving her only enough awareness to know what he was doing to her just about sent him over the edge. He collapsed onto the mat next to her bound body muttering "Adele…"

After catching his breath, Melvin looked over at Green Eyes to see her staring at him with eyes of fire. He laughed at her, then got up and proceeded to clean himself, then her, as much as she would let him.

He had thought about going out for another pet that night, but instead, he considered the force with which he had climaxed when thinking of Mother. He decided then and there that he would wait. It was early evening now; he would go about their normal routine of eating, bathing, then tucking in the pets. Then, in the morning, he would do it.

He gave Green Eyes yet another pill, this time one big enough to knock her out for a while, at least until supper, then he secured her door and went to Princess' cell. She was curled up in a ball weeping, but when she saw him there, she reached out her hand as if to ask him for help.

He chuckled and entered her cell, pulling a hanky out of his pocket as he went. Kneeling down beside her mat, Melvin began to wipe the tears from her eyes, then he combed his fingers through her scraggly hair in a failing attempt to straighten it. She was so very beautiful. As far as looks went, she was a perfect specimen, and for that would remain his favorite.

But Princess lacked in the sex department, that was for sure. The screaming and struggling were great, but the last time he "indulged her" all she did was cry and sob. He barely enjoyed himself and left her cell wanting to kick the life out of her. But that wasn't the way a good master treated his pets.

Green Eyes, on the other hand, was a fighter. Oh, just the thought of what he had just done to her, the way she bled and the way she took the solid punch to the back of her head, in the beginning, just to get him going, made his member jump in his pants. But he had to admit, while he liked her feistiness, and would use her often, it wasn't Green Eyes that got such a wonderful result. It had been the thought of Mother.

He kissed Princess on the temple and assured her that he would be back with supper, then he went to Mother's cell. Opening the door, he entered and sat in the folding chair in the corner so he could watch her. She turned to him right away, and he saw the lustful look in her eye. Though her mind and body weren't working together, he saw that she had her hand between her legs and was clumsily trying to rub herself, to no avail. Melvin smiled as he watched her, then noticed that she was smiling back at him. She opened her mouth and gurgled something he couldn't understand, spit falling from the corner of her lips. Yes, she wanted him alright, and tomorrow he was going to do it. He was going to give Mother a thrusting like she had never known, and for all her damaged brain cells, wouldn't soon forget.

"Don't worry, horrid Adele," he leered. "You're next. In the morning I will show you what you've been missing." Adele's smile grew, and she rubbed harder as the cackling began.

It was turning out that Melvin Frink was his mother's son after all.

∞

John Torrey held the phone's receiver up to his ear with his shoulder and wrote furiously on his tablet. On the phone was Dr. Philip Arondale, side-stepping his questions with vague, superficial answers about Adele and Melvin Frink. Torrey wanted to reach through the phone and strangle him, but instead simply noted what the man did say, if it applied to the case at all, and most of it wasn't.

Arondale claimed that he was primarily Mrs. Frink's shrink, and had been for decades. He stated that he had been trying to get ahold of her, but she could not be reached, and he chalked it up to the fact that he had ducked out on an appointment due to a patient emergency. As for Melvin, he claimed he had conferred with Meadows Community physicians at the specific request of Mrs. Frink regarding a procedure performed to lessen the negative side effects of his brain injury, but he wasn't at liberty to reveal any more than that. Torrey asked him if he had followed up with Melvin or knew what his state of mind had been since his release from the hospital, and it was then that Arondale became anxious to get off the line. He simply said that he was no longer in charge of the patient in any manner after he went home. His mother hired a nurse and saw to follow-up care, which he knew nothing about. Now he claimed he was late for an appointment, terribly late, and really couldn't talk any more.

The snotty man was pissing Torrey off. "Doctor, I need you to come to the campus station for an interview. When are you available?" He wanted to see the man's face and eyes when they spoke because he was certain he was hiding something.

"Is that really necessary?" Arondale asked nervously. "My schedule is -"

"Yes, it is, sir. This is a police investigation. If you aren't able to get here, I can come to you."

The doctor, after hem-hawing around, sighed and said, "I can be there at two-thirty this afternoon, but I can only give you about a half-hour. And I will not break patient privilege; have I made myself clear?"

Torrey didn't answer the question. "See you then," he replied, then abruptly hung up. If the guy didn't show, he was going right to his office and calling baloney to his uptight face.

Torrey made a note and stuck it to the front of his notebook, then looked at the clock. It was nearly eleven, and by the way, his stomach was growling, it was time to find out what Manning had learned from Mrs. Frink, and they should do it over lunch.

He stood up from his desk and turned around to find Manning right behind him, making him nearly mess his pants.

"Manning! What the heck?"

"Sorry," the young officer replied sheepishly. "I just wanted to let you know that I'm pretty hungry; wanna get a bite and go over this then?"

Embarrassed at being startled, Torrey looked around to make sure that no one had seen him jump, then he grabbed his notebook from his desk. "Yeah, that's what I was thinking."

In the car, Manning started first while Torrey maneuvered the campus squad car out of the police lot. "Okay, I tried the Frink home phone number four times, at intervals. The first three times all I got was a machine, but the last time someone picked up. They didn't say anything, just listened at first. Then they said hello. I introduced myself and asked for the lady of the house, but the guy said she was unavailable. I asked who he was and he said he was the houseman. When I asked where she was, the guy said she didn't inform him of her comings and goings unless it pertained to his job in some way. He assumed she was doing some charity work or was seeing her physician, but he didn't know."

"Did you get the guy's name?"

Manning nodded. "Yeah... um... Astley. Reginald Astley. He had a British accent, but I gotta tell you, from the Brits I've encountered here on campus, and as you know, there are several, it sounded forced to me. But what do I know? I told him I had a matter of official business to discuss with her regarding some of her son's belongings being found in campus storage. Astley got kind of excited then. He asked what the items were, and I told him that campus policy didn't allow us to divulge student information over the phone, and when could I come to bring the stuff. He said he would have her get back to me and took my number. He sounded kind of upset, to tell you the truth."

"Well, these rich people make those poor butlers do everything; he probably thinks he's in for a bitching." Torrey pulled into the lot and got into the long line at the drive-thru. "No time she might be home?"

Manning shook his head. "Nah. He said he's worked for her for ten years and he hardly ever sees her unless it's in passing. I tried to call a couple of the charities listed in the file on Frink, but they both said that Adele hadn't been participating in the organization of events for some time... since her son had fallen ill. The woman at the second place, The Baltimore Historical Society, actually said she hadn't seen her in weeks, though she has tried to phone. After that, the trail goes cold. I should have asked for the son."

"No, Cohen's right," Torrey replied as he advanced the car about three inches. "We don't want to freak the guy out."

"So, what about you?"

Torrey cleared his throat and gestured toward his notebook, which sat up on the dashboard. "I spoke to Dr. Arondale. Wow, is this guy evasive. He danced around most of my questions and used a bunch of professional lingo while he hid behind confidentiality, but I think he knows something. I'm not sure what, but I could feel his anxiety through the phone. Probably he thinks we're trying to shake him down for over-prescribing meds, who knows. Anyway, I practically had to threaten to come to his office to get him to agree to come down for a face-to-face. He's due at two-thirty, and if he doesn't show up, we're gonna hound dog him, you hear?"

"Sounds good to me."

The two men got their food and parked in the corner of the lot to eat. They discussed Cohen and Miller and wondered what kind of stuff those two had come up with at Meadows Community. The two were due back for a meeting at one, and both Torrey and Manning felt like that seemed like it was an eternity away. When they finished their food, Torrey suggested that they visit a couple of Frink's professors who were still on staff so they could get a feel for the guy... at least, the guy he had been before a piece of a building fell on his head.

They pulled out of the lot and headed back to campus; the first person they were going to visit was the head of neuro-psychiatric surgery, Professor Stanton.

R.W.K. Clark

CHAPTER 15

Melvin had been the one who answered the phone when Manning called mid-morning. The fact was that he did it strictly out of habit; it rang, and he answered it. But as soon as he had the receiver to his ear, he knew he had made a mistake; the missing girls were all over the news… at least, Princess and Candy were. So far he hadn't seen anything about Green Eyes, and he figured that he wouldn't for at least a day or two. Leaving campus had been a great decision, and going into the bar had been a magnificent one. Sure, he liked them classy and educated, but the fact was girls like that were loved. Girls like Green Eyes? Well, sometimes they weren't missed for years.

At first, after picking up the phone, he said nothing, and then he realized how dangerous his silence could be. Without even thinking he created the British houseman Reginald Astley, and the guy seemed to take over without missing a beat. Just as he suspected, it had been a cop; a campus cop, but a cop none the less. The first two girls had been students, so, of course, the campus police would be in on the investigation. Had the cop he ran into at Eisenhower Library somehow managed to connect the dots? If so, how had he done it? Melvin had spoken to literally no one but the library cop and his pets when he left home on the hunt; he just couldn't believe they were onto him already.

But when the cop, an Officer Manning, asked for his mother with some trumped up story about having found some of "her son's" belongings in storage, Melvin became fairly convinced that somehow they were on to him. He lived at home, as he had his entire life, and throughout his time at Johns Hopkins. He kept absolutely nothing at the campus; he carried all he needed with him from home to school and from school to home for each and every class and lecture and study group. The man was lying. Why would he want to speak with Adele? Why not Melvin? He hadn't been killed in his accident, and he was pretty sure all pertinent staff, including the associate of the cop on the phone he had met at Eisenhower, knew he was alive and able to function.

The guy was fishing, no more and no less.

He had gotten rid of him easily enough, and only for now. Melvin was sure they would call back, and eventually, they would pay a visit to the house. But the good thing about living behind thick walls and iron gates was the fact that if one wanted to get at you, all you had to do was deny access. He knew that without a warrant, they couldn't just climb the wall and arrest him. They would have to have a warrant, and without evidence, they couldn't get one. The best part was that any evidence couldn't be found unless they got inside.

They were running like hamsters in a cage, feeling their way in the darkness like a blind man who simply couldn't find the light switch, groping... groping.

So, for now, he and his lovelies were safe from the infiltrators, but he was more convinced than ever that he should put off looking for the next addition to his collection indefinitely. That didn't matter though. He had enough food and supplies on the property to keep him and his pets comfortable indefinitely. It was a massive place, and Mother had seen to it that they were not only prepared for life in general, but for any kind of emergency imaginable. She had been a paranoid sort, always buying into the "end of the world" theories that came from watching too much television. Yes, he and the pets had more than enough to hole up for a while.

The only real disappointment about the cop's call was the fact that Melvin was a creature of strict routine; it was wired deep within him by his mother, practically from birth. She had drilled the importance of consistency into him in ways that his mind had chosen to block out, but her methods had gotten the job done, and this morning when Officer Friendly called, he had just finished getting the girls ready for the day, feeding them and dressing them. All except for Mother, of course. He had fed her, but instead of dressing her he had given her a thorough cleaning and douching, which she sickeningly seemed to enjoy. Truth be told, he had enjoyed it too. While he carried it out, he had placed her hand on himself, and she had been more than happy to do so; in addition, she clumsily touched herself with her free hand. She grunted, and her eyes rolled back into her head from the pleasure. Melvin couldn't wait to fully indulge himself.

But while he bathed her, and while she touched him, he began to experience recall like never before, even before his accident. Flashes of his childhood came to him in sharp, lightning-fast images that disappeared as quickly as they came. In one, his mother had him tied to the foot of his bed, and she had him in her mouth. She was biting it fairly hard, and it hurt, but he could remember. In yet another flash, he was on his knees before her, and they both were naked. He shook this memory away, but in his gut, he recalled what she was making him do, and she was striking him with a riding crop across the back as he did so.

Now, here she was before him and having just pleasured herself while he "served" her by bathing her, he found himself infuriated. Scared that he may beat her to death then and there, he had left her and gone upstairs to get his wits about him. He didn't want her dead, but he did want to violate what was left of her brains, and he wanted to do it over and over again.

He had just been on his way back down to the cellar with a bag in hand when the phone had rung.

But now the call was over, and he could shift his focus back to what was important: the training of Queen Adele. He had a bag with him in one hand that held a clean sock and tape to gag her. It also held lubricant, handcuffs, and piano wire, which would bind her feet. It would cut her severely, and he looked forward to watching her bleed with gusto. He hoped she cried, but he knew deep inside that she wouldn't. Adele Frink was a classic sadist, and she had been even when her husband was alive. When father had tired of her sick games, Adele had used Melvin for her playtoy. Now it was his turn.

At the bottom of the cellar stairs, he noticed how still it was: no sound but three uneven sets of breathing. Mother was likely sleeping, but that wouldn't last long, because he would see to it. As for Princess and Green Eyes, he had two pills that he planned to give them, so he didn't have to listen to their screaming and crying and fighting. At the bottom of the stairs, Melvin closed the door securely; setting the bag on the floor, he fished the pills out of his breast pocket and looked them over. Yes, this would send the others to la-la land, alright.

Quietly, Melvin crept down the concrete corridor in his stocking feet. He glanced in at Mother as he passed her cell; she was napping, her hand still between her legs. Princess was lying on her left side, staring at the far wall where his chair was located. She caught his movement out of the corner of her eye and jumped slightly, she quickly closed her eyes and pretended to sleep. Melvin sat down on the mat next to her, tucked one pill into his pocket, and held the other.

"I know you're awake, Princess," he said softly. "I saw you close your eyes when I came in. Well, I have a treat for you. You have been such a good girl that I am going to treat you to some yummy night-night medicine. It will send you to dreamland. Don't worry; I won't be needing your services tonight. I have much bigger plans, plans that have been a long time in coming."

In only seconds, Melvin gave Sarah Russell the pill, and in a few minutes, she was snoring lightly. He took her pulse, listened to her heart, and made sure she was not faking before tucking her securely beneath her blankets and turning off the overhead light. A nightlight, plugged in across the room, gave her plenty of light to see if she should wake.

After, he went to Green Eyes. As usual, she was rolling around, fighting against the padded restraints which he had replaced with the rope, but they were too much for her. There was intelligence in her eyes, and he knew she was watching and waiting and looking for him to slip up ever so slightly. This one had to be watched really close.

"Green Eyes, my dear, relax. I am here only to give you a pill: your favorite. You'll sleep like a baby until morning, and don't worry about me using you tonight. I have another... date."

As soon as she heard the word pill, Green Eyes went limp, and she looked up at him longingly. Melvin knelt down and gave it to her. Within minutes, the pill carried her away to where she wanted to be.

It was time.

Now, Melvin went out and put some music on low on the small stereo, playing lightly. He moved it closer to his mother's cell, causing her to stir, but not wake completely. Then he peeled off the turtle-neck he was wearing and tossed it toward the cellar door. Next, he fetched the bag of goodies, which also included some fine household items that he thought would fit nicely in her orifices, and he let himself into her cell. As he unpacked the bag, Mother woke with curious grunts and groans.

Melvin slowly and methodically laid out all of his toys on the metal table and pushed it near her mat. Next, he knelt down and shoved the balled up sock into her mouth, then proceeded to wrap a long strip of tape around her head to secure it. She looked at him with fear in her eyes, but Melvin also saw a glint of pleasure. He quickly cuffed her, then bound her ankles with the piano wire; he pulled it tight, so it cut into her skin, watching her face the whole time. But Mother didn't shed a tear. Instead, Melvin could have sworn her eyes were smiling.

"Oh, yes, Adele... it's my turn now..."

∞

A sense of deja vu came over John Torrey as he and his three cohorts took their seats in the conference room, the same seats they had been sitting in since the day before. Each was opening notebooks or tablets and shuffling papers as they poised their pens for writing. Time to compare notes.

"So, men, where are we?" Cohen began by asking. "Miller and I learned some things that I think you'll find interesting, but we'll start with you in a minute; I am interested in what you got from Adele Frink. But first, I think you should know that after we left here, we stopped at the station to run both of the Frinks through the computer... we ended up with nothing but basic public information... house, cars, divorce, the birth of the boy, etc. They've got money alright... looks like the father left them double-digit millions, and there is likely more tucked away somewhere. Anyway, aside from that we got some bad news while we were there."

Torrey looked up expectantly; now what?

Miller took over. "A call came into my desk... we have another missing girl. Denise Hoskins, twenty-four, lives over in the flats with her best friend, Karen Walker. It was the Walker girl who called in. She says the two of them were at a bar over by where the Cambridge Apartments used to be, a place called 'The Thirsty Irishman,' a dive hangout for locals. Anyway, Walker says they were there with a couple male acquaintances who were playing darts, and that the last thing she knew, she was sitting at the bar with Hoskins, but she said she must have had too much because she passed out. When she woke, one of the male friends was rousing her to take her home, and Denise was gone. When she asked where the girl went, one of the guys told her she left with a taller, slender guy, kind of dorky-looking, with slightly receding blond hair. He was wearing jeans and a t-shirt with some logo on it... it was white or beige. Anyway, she asked the guys to make sure Walker got home alright and told them she was going to party, and to tell Karen she'd see her in the morning. When Karen woke at nine-thirty this morning Denise wasn't home. She said she wouldn't have thought anything of it, but when she tried to call the girl to have her bring home a little of the 'dog that bit her,' all she got was the cell provider's message stating that the customer could not receive calls at that time.

"Now, I gave Miss Walker my cell number and told her to call us when Denise got home. It's one fifteen now, and no word. With the prior cases on our plate, I think it would be wise to consider her girl number three, don't you?"

Torrey rubbed both of his hands over his face then through his sparse hair. "This guy's on a roll."

Miller nodded. "Looks that way. That's why after I took the report, we headed over and had a talk with the two male friends... they both confirmed the story and gave the same description of the guy. The only thing that doesn't fit Frink is that in his school photos he is always wearing thick tortoise shell-type glasses. The men say this guy had no glasses on at all."

"Contacts," Manning muttered. "Did anyone see a white van by chance?"

Both of the city boys shook their heads. "That's neither here nor there anymore," Cohen suggested. "With the kind of money the Frinks have, he's liable to have access to all kinds of cars. Oh, speaking of which, Frink doesn't have a license anywhere in the US, so we put out an all-points-bulletin for any vehicle registered to Adele Frink. It should be stopped right away, and the driver brought in for questioning, no matter who it is."

Miller took over then. "Anyway, when we left the two guys, we headed over to Meadows Community and had a talk with Dr. Fitzsimmons. The guy was as nervous as a chicken in a fox's den; it just didn't make sense. We told him we were there because Mr. Frink had 'gone missing,' and his mother wasn't in any shape to deal with it. We learned some pretty shocking facts from this dude, let me tell you."

"Like what?" Torrey asked hesitantly; he wasn't sure how much more weirdness he could take.

Cohen replied, "For starters, Adele Frink has donated a substantial amount of money to the hospital's neurosurgery unit. It seems that since that was Melvin's area of study, and since he suffered a brain injury, she felt it was only right to further the cause. But the truth of the matter was far worse. Fitzsimmons didn't want to tell us at first, but when I got up and told Miller to wait for me while I got a warrant, he changed his tune. First, he told us to get ready to arrest him when he was through because he had been involved in some bad trouble when it came to the Frink case." Cohen paused, rubbed his forehead, and sat back with a sigh.

Torrey and Manning waited, but Manning lost his patience. "Well? Like what kind of trouble?"

Miller took over. "It turns out that Adele Frink didn't donate the money to the hospital out of the goodness of her heart. She did it as payment to entice Fitzsimmons to perform a lobotomy on her son, with Dr. Arondale right alongside him, pulling the puppet strings."

The room fell completely silent for what seemed like forever. The men all just stared at each other... Cohen and Miller with expressions that said, "I know, right?", and Torrey and Manning with looks that screamed "What!" After several moments, Torrey asked the gratuitous question.

"Aren't lobotomies illegal in the United States?"

Cohen snorted and shook his head in disgust. "They're supposed to be. Anyway, Mrs. Frink's precious boy had been planning to specialize in psychiatric neurosurgery, and he had spoken often with her about the lobotomization procedures of the past. It seems he believed that they could somehow be perfected and put to good use, with further study. Anyway, these conversations had his mom convinced that was all he needed to come out of his coma and get back to normal. Fitzsimmons also mentioned that it seemed to him that Adele had a somewhat unhealthy attachment to the boy, and would go to any length to bring him back to her. When they recommended ending life support at one point, she began to prepare to bring him home. That was when she basically bribed them to do the procedure secretly. It was all very hush-hush. By the way, Fitzsimmons is being booked into the county, along with three other members of his team. Now we just have to get our hands on Arondale; any luck with him?"

Torrey took a breath and opened his notebook. "I spoke with him this morning. He's evasive, passive-aggressive, and fond of hiding behind patient/doctor privilege. He admitted to overseeing Frink's psych care during his recovery, but his admission was extremely limited. According to him, he cares for Adele alone, and only treated the boy at her request. He mentioned a "procedure," and when I tried to delve deeper, he dodged me. He was hiding something, and I got the feeling it was more than the Frink's psych histories. I told him he needed to come in for a face-to-face; he dodged some more, and I mentioned warrants and judges. He'll be here at two-thirty, supposedly. If he doesn't show up, I'm gonna go to his office, then I'm gonna park in front of his house until he starts peeking out the window. This guy knows more than anyone, I'm sure of it, and after listening to you, I wouldn't be surprised if he was the conductor of this whole rotten orchestra."

Miller glanced at his cell phone screen. "It's nearly two now, so let's go over what we want to ask him. If he's in the mix, we need to catch him up in it, that's for sure, so let's make sure we ask the right questions and snare the bastard in his own net. What kind of shrink covers up for a lobotomy, much less goes along with it or condones it?"

"A sicko," Cohen said as he clicked open his ballpoint, "that's who. Come on guys, let's get our act together; I wanna be ready for this guy."

CHAPTER 16

Melvin sat in his mother's cell, his knees pulled up to his chest, his arms wrapped tightly around them. He had a smile on his face, his eyes were glossed over, and his hair was a mess. He felt happier and more content than he ever had in his life.

His mother was on her mat, sleeping soundly. Her nose had dried and had crusted blood around the nostrils, and the left side of her face was swollen and bruised. There was a bloody bite mark on her left breast. Her legs were spread wide, and her privates were swollen and red to the point that they were almost purple. Beneath her was a streak of blood on the sheet, and the thought made him smile even wider. Even as she slept, Adele Frink was smiling. She had loved every minute of it, and she had fought him, knowing that it brought him great satisfaction, just as he knew that each punch and bite brought the same satisfaction to her.

He couldn't take his eyes off of her. His mind was on her aged beauty and ugliness, which seemed to meld together into a symphony of perfection. As he admired her drooping form, his mind wandered to his other pets. What a waste of time they had been; such horrible risks he had taken in taking them and bringing them here, to the refuge his mother had made for them both. He thought he wanted them because she had kept him from sex and living for so long, but now he knew that all he had ever needed was Adele. She was everything. He knew that he had to get rid of them, get them out of this house before it was too late, and he was more thankful than ever for the crematory. Because of it, disposal would be easy, and he felt no remorse at the thought whatsoever. After all, it had been a very pleasurable learning experience, and it was one he would never regret. Neither of them mattered anyway. Their family and friends would go on with their lives, just as Melvin would, only he would do it with Adele, his beautiful pet, his intoxicating slave.

As he thought about Princess and Green Eyes, he continued to stare at his mother, the thought of being completely alone with her forever and ever. He neither saw anything around him nor heard the slightest noise. But there were noises, and they were coming from Green Eyes' cell down the hall.

∞

While he had been raping his own mother, Green Eyes had tried to block the sounds with her small pillow. She had wanted to vomit; she had met some psychos in her time, but this one took the cake. Not only had he drilled into her head and done something that made her much slower all the way around, but he was raping her, the girl next door, and his very own mom, who, by the way, sounded like she loved every minute of it. What had she gotten herself into?

So, Green Eyes had lain on her mat and studied the room while she covered her ears. The guy was good; he had kept things in the cell to a bare minimum, but there were definitely things she could use as a weapon. The most obvious involved the metal table and the folding chair. The chair would be difficult to get apart, without tools of some kind, but the metal table was old, very old, and rusty. From where she was lying, it seemed that the single steel pole that held up the table's flat surface was just sitting loosely inside of a hole in the base. As a matter of fact, she had seen the table wobble every time he brushed against it or grabbed a towel or water off it. If she could get her hands on that pole...

Right then she heard a noise through her pillow, an odd noise that was close by and didn't fit in with the screams of pleasure from down the corridor. She removed the pillow from her ear and looked to the right. Was she seeing things? Could it really be true? He had given her a pretty good pill, but she had been using dope for years, so that wasn't what was causing her to see what she thought she saw.

The door to the cell had come unlatched and slipped open; somehow he had not gotten the bolt to slide in all the way when he locked it.

Green Eyes, with stiff, painful joints, got to her hands and knees. A wave of nausea came over her, and she quickly buried her head in her pillow and puked. She hoped that door was really open, or she was going to have to sleep in that.

In nothing but her nightshirt, she began to slowly and laboriously crawl off her mat and toward the door. One foot, two, and then she was close enough to see; the door had indeed unlatched and slipped open slightly, just a crack.

The moaning and screaming and punching continued. That so-and-so must really hate his mother; Green Eyes could hear every slap and punch, but the woman didn't cry. The screams she heard were those of pleasure, which was fine with her. She hoped they kept at it for another hour. It also helped that the music was playing.

Changing directions, Green Eyes crept on her knobby knees toward the metal table. She sat up on her knees, wincing in pain as she did so, and grasped the small table top. Moving very, very slowly, and peeling her ears as she went, Green Eyes began to turn the tabletop; it was definitely loose! If only she could pull herself up, then she could stand on the base and pull off the top. Voila! A heavy weapon to be reckoned with.

She turned to the chair; maybe she could pull it over and sit on it, put her feet on the table's base, and that would give her enough leverage to pull off the top. No, it wouldn't work, she thought. Moving the metal chair across the concrete floor would make far too much noise, and she wouldn't dare risk it.

Then she saw it.

Right next to the chair, in the crack where the wall met the floor, was an old syringe. Somehow he hadn't noticed it. She moved so fast that she nearly fell on her face in her weakened state, but she forced her doped up, malnourished arms to hold her up and pull her forward. Progress was slow, but, at last, she made it to the syringe.

Grabbing it up, Green Eyes took off the cap, and when she saw that the needle was intact and had not been broken off, she could have cried with relief. It was more of a miracle than she would have dared ask for, but here it was her miracle.

The plunger pulled back easily, sliding as if the syringe had never been used. She pumped it in and out several times, then pulled it back one final time, leaving it nearly full of air. Slowly and gently she recapped it and made her way back to her bed and her pillow full of puke. She paid no attention to the stench-exuding pile; instead, she turned it over, used a dirty towel to cover it and then laid her head where her feet usually went with her blanket wadded up to support her head. She lay there quietly, on her back, staring at the ceiling with a smile on her face and an air-filled syringe in her hand, hidden by her right thigh.

Ken, or whoever he was, was going to be in for a big surprise.

The screaming had continued, then stopped, and now she lay there in the silence wondering what her captor was doing, what was taking him so long to get to her and clean her up for bed. She didn't know he was entranced by his sleeping mother and the painful, rotten sex he had just had with her. Green Eyes had no idea that she and Princess, for the time being, were forgotten as the lunatic who took them replayed scenes with his mother over and over in his head.

But he would come eventually, and when he did, she was going to drive eighty CCs of air directly into his neck and hope for the best. Maybe she would stick it in his eye and plunge it into his brain. Either way, he was going down, and she was getting out of that dungeon.

∞

Dr. Philip Arondale sat alone in the conference room at the Johns Hopkins Campus Police station. Before him on the table sat a steaming cup of black coffee, but he had taken only a single sip. It was awful, tasting like watered down mud with grounds floating in it. What did he expect? He couldn't expect commoners such as these to know what real coffee was, now could he?

Across from him was a two-way mirror, which he looked into often and admired his reflection, or straightened his hair, or simply practiced looking calm. On the other side of the mirror were John Torrey, Nick Manning, and city cops Cohen and Miller. They stood in a row, arms crossed over their chests, watching his demeanor and studying him. They knew much more about his involvement in the Frink coma case than he realized; if he had, he would have been pacing the room crying and dialing his cell phone like mad. But for now, he was there to simply answer a few innocent questions about his lover, Adele Frink, and the accident her son had gone through a few years back. Easy... he could do it standing on his head and be out in time to make it to his three-thirty tennis match.

Torrey and his pals wanted him to sweat things for a bit. He maintained his calm demeanor for about fifteen more minutes, then he began to fidget with the coffee cup. That lasted two minutes, and then Arondale stood up and began to pace back and forth, looking anxiously over his shoulder at the door, as though the cops would walk through it any second.

Finally, they did. One by one the big, gruff cops filed into the room and told Arondale to sit before taking their own chairs. Each of them carried either notebooks or file folders; one of them had a laptop bag hanging over his shoulder, which he emptied as soon as he sat down and booted the computer that had been stored inside of it.

Torrey began. "Dr. Arondale, I'm Officer Torrey of Johns Hopkins Campus Police... we spoke earlier on the phone. Do you know why I asked you to come in?"

Arondale shrugged arrogantly. "I assume you wanted more information than what I was able to give you during the call. Before we go any further, I just want to remind you about -"

"Patient confidentiality," Miller interjected. "Yeah, yeah, we get it."

Cohen had started typing furiously, but then he paused. "Dr. Arondale, how long have you been in charge of Adele Frink's psychiatric care?"

Philip shrugged again, this time with a more thoughtful look on his face. "I'd say close to thirty years."

"So, that would have put you in Boston prior to the death of her husband," Cohen mused. "Does that sound about right?"

He nodded. "Yes. Actually, I started my practice in Boston, and I only moved here at Adele's request after the death of Melvin's father." He knit his brow as if he were considering what he would reveal very carefully before continuing. "You see, Adele is a fragile sort. Her diagnosis requires a very specific combination of medications in order for her to be functionally balanced on a consistent basis. This requires close monitoring, and when she first moved here, she found that local psychiatrists were more interested in brushing off her diagnoses and changing her medications. This led to very... unpleasant consequences, both for Adele and her son. Eventually, she called me and practically begged me to relocate. I refused until she agreed to fund my new practice until I got on my feet."

Manning chuckled, his cynicism shining through in the question he asked. "And you were so worried about the poor woman that you just dumped all your Boston patients and came running, right?"

Arondale smirked. "Something like that, but it's a bit more detailed than you let on with your naiveté. Yes, I came at Adele's request, and while I was concerned for her mental state, I was more concerned for... well, let's just say I was worried about what the consequences would be if I didn't get her stabilized."

Miller asked, "So, would you say she is stabilized now?"

"I would say that, for a woman of her age with the diagnoses she has, she is about as stable and functional as is humanly possible." Arondale's eyes shifted, and then he looked down at his hands; the men knew he was lying.

"Okay, so you can't reveal her diagnosis," Torrey said. "Let us speak hypothetically then, sir. If any random person on the street had the same diagnosis, and this person was either not taking their medication, or they were taking it incorrectly, what symptoms would manifest?"

Arondale put on his doctor's cap and began to rub his chin; the man loved to show off his intellect, it was obvious. "Well, for starters, they would go from very active states to deep depressive states at the drop of a hat. Spending binges are not uncommon, and neither is promiscuity. Some become horribly abusive to those around them for no reason at all, and they may become violent. Healthy relationships are almost impossible without years of successful treatment coming first. Any relationships that are formed typically end up in a clinging obsession that can cause damage to the object of their affection. Many times, these people, when left unmedicated, will self-medicate through the use of illicit substances. The list goes on and on."

Torrey continued. "Adele demonstrated some of these symptoms then?" When Arondale hesitated, he stated, "Before you answer, you should know that we currently have a court order for Adele's records with you, as well as those of her son, Melvin. Please, just cooperate. There are missing women involved in the case we are working on."

Suddenly, Arondale sat forward, shock and concern shadowing his face instantly. "Are you referring to the missing students? You certainly don't think..."

"Just answer the question, sir," Torrey continued. "You see, we know that you not only treated Adele Frink, but that you treated her son on occasion, but we'll get to that later. I will assume that Mrs. Frink exhibited most or all of the symptoms you mentioned, and bearing that in mind, I will ask you this: how long have the two of you been sleeping together?"

Arondale's mouth dropped open, and he feigned shock, though poorly. "You dare to insult me? I am an ethical man who has practiced in my field, with commendations, for decades. Behavior such as you are suggesting would be a travesty of trust; it would be criminal."

Cohen shook his head. "Then you're a criminal. How long have you been doing it? Since before her husband died, or only since she funded your Baltimore practice?"

The doctor stared at the lieutenant with a determined look that slowly, but surely, faded away into one of defeat. "Since Boston. You have to understand, Adele is a very beautiful woman, but it was more than that. Once she got her hooks into me I was trapped; she had the goods on me, and she had the money. I was stuck. And... There were worse circumstances involved, and I convinced myself that by sleeping with her I would be able to curb the... horrible behaviors that she was exhibiting. Please know that I tried to end that part of the relationship, to go back to the professional interaction we once had, but it was too late."

"And the pills?" Cohen continued. "How long have you been over-prescribing controlled substances at her every whim?"

Arondale sighed with defeat. "Since I saw her downtown trying to score drugs from a prostitute. I wanted to keep her off the street, to keep her home with Melvin being the mother she should be. I thought..."

"Well," Torrey interrupted, "Whatever you thought, you thought wrong. You just put a band-aid on her bullet wound; that was all. Now, I want to go back to this "horrible" behavior that having sex with her was supposed to eliminate. Was she out hooking? Was she swinging? How bad could it have been that you thought it was okay to take her to bed for any reason?"

Suddenly, the clean-cut, well-dressed man slumped in his chair, and the four men across from him knew he was about to begin to spill the real beans. The look on his face told them that he knew it was time to pay the piper and that he had always known this day would come. The man realized that it was best not to fight it. He took a deep breath and began to tell them the whole story, confidentiality be damned.

"Adele Frink was brought to me by her husband more than thirty years ago in Boston. She was young, but her illness was manifesting, and the poor man didn't know what to do. He was extremely wealthy and powerful, but he was busy. Because of this, he needed her home caring for their home and preparing for the family they had planned to have. But one minute she was crying, the next she was walking on rays of sunshine, and the next minute she was beating the life out of him while he slept. She ran up atrocious bills and hid them from him, even though he could afford anything she wanted. She would disappear for weeks at a time, then call him, begging for forgiveness, depressed and angry at herself. Melvin's father was at the end of his rope. He loved her very much, but in addition to that, he needed her straightened out for the sake of his reputation and the reputation of his company, which had been in his family for five generations.

"I diagnosed her as manic depressive with schizophrenic tendencies. I put her on the very best medications available for the times and began seeing her three times per week, but that wasn't until we put her in the mental unit at Boston University for six months. We got her stabilized, discharged her, and got her therapy and med monitoring on a roll. It all went well for about a year, then another episode came. She had stopped taking her meds three months prior. We got her well again after another hospitalization, then it all went again, just like before. This cycle continued, over and over, until he caught her in bed with Melvin when he was just seven. She had not only been having sex with the boy, but she had also been practicing her sadistic tastes on him. He had enough and told her he was having her put in prison. He disappeared shortly after and was found floating in the river soon after that. I knew that she did it, but her money was the taproot for my practice, and she threatened to pull it and run with the boy if I said anything. She also demanded sex, and I gave it to her, along with all the dope she wanted, if she promised to leave the boy alone. She promised, but I couldn't tell you if she ever did. All I can tell you for sure is that for his entire life, at least, as long as I've known him, he was utterly and completely controlled by her. As far as I know, he never even knew the joy of having a driver's license."

Arondale went quiet, and a single tear trickled down his cheek.

They let him have a moment of silence while he processed the truth that he had been hiding for thirty years. The truth that he had been ignoring for the sake of money, a thriving practice and a regular piece of mentally ill, sick, perverted relations. Manning shoved a box of tissue across the table at him, and he took one with a nod of thanks, shame keeping him from looking the young man in the face. After several minutes, he continued.

"Then, when Melvin had his accident a few years back, Adele seemed to regain some of her youthful focus. Here was her son, who she allowed to study a subject he was passionate about due to how sick his mother truly was, and when he attended school, he was out from under her thumb. I don't know if she knew it or not, but he had this crazy idea that he could study the history and techniques of the frontal lobotomy, and he could then perfect it somehow. You know, figure out where all the Neuropsychologists of the past had screwed up, where they had missed it, and rectify it. Then, and only then, would he be able to turn his mother's life around for her. He talked to her about it constantly, though she denied the need for any real help. She did listen, and I suppose she was proud of how accomplished he was in his studies. As proud as a person like Adele could be, anyway. So, she let him go, but she despised it, and she spent more time whining to me about it and popping pills than Melvin will ever know. Then the accident came, and the coma, and he was under her thumb again, where he belonged. Don't get me wrong, she didn't want him in a coma, hooked up to machines. She wanted him home with her, where they could "always be together." He didn't need school or friends, or girls or sports. All he needed was her. But Adele needed him out of that coma, and no matter how much money she spent, no matter what doctors did, and no matter how much she waited and fretted over his frozen body and mind, she couldn't change things. Adele Frink was powerless."

He paused, took a drink of the ice cold coffee that had been sitting there since he arrived, grimaced, and set it down. Cohen turned to Miller and told him to get the man a fresh one, but Arondale asked for water instead. Miller left the conference room, and the doctor continued.

"She came to me after he had been in the coma

three years and five months. During a regular session which consisted of nothing but her talking about her beloved Melvin, and how they wanted to pull the plug. Oh, she wasn't having that at all; if it cost her entire fortune, Adele would wait it out. But that day she told me she didn't want to wait anymore. I... I didn't know what she meant at first, then she started to ramble on about Melvin and his obsession with the perfection of the lobotomization procedure, how he loved her so much that he had chosen finding a way to fix her as his life's mission. She owed him, she said. Not for the years of abuse or rape or for the fact that she had his father killed, but she owed him because he had given her his life in its entirety.

"That was when she offered me ten million dollars, free and clear, to meet with Fitzsimmons and his team and convince them to conduct a frontal cortex stimulation and lobotomy... money was no object. She would pay each member of his team a generous amount upon their signing of a confidentiality agreement, and she would fund the new neuropsych wing at Meadows Memorial. Adele Frink had no idea what she was asking, but I did, and I tried to argue and reason, but she was never one to understand the reason of any kind... she was, and is, insane. She didn't care what they did, as far as the method of lobotomization they chose. She didn't care who did it. What she cared about was only two things: that I made it happen and supervised and advised, and that her son would wake up and go home with her."

Torrey leaned forward, horrified. "Didn't you tell her the history behind this procedure? Didn't you warn her of the potential outcome? What if the kid had come out a vegetable?"

Suddenly, Arondale burst out in laughter that was almost hysterical, and it lasted for several minutes. When he finally gained control of himself again, he took a drink of the water Miller had brought, wiped his mouth, but continued to smile.

"Of course I did," he spat through his grin. "I gave her the grim details of case studies, I showed her photographs, I begged her and pleaded with her. I told her that death was better than what he would likely be in the end. She didn't care... Adele wanted a vegetable son to take home and care for and rape for the rest of her life behind the big gates that surround the fortress they live in. So, I did it. I took the proposal to Fitzsimmons, along with a stack of checks and contracts and Adele's lawyer, and I convinced them to do it. It wasn't hard, believe me. To them, it was like playing doctor as a child again. 'Let's cut this guy's head open and see what happens!' It was a joke.

"But, true to my word, I did supervise and advise during the surgery, and I demanded the stimulatory probe in hopes that it would bring him out of the coma, vegetable or not. I planned to get him home, continue to provide Adele and Melvin with whatever psych drugs they may need, and otherwise cut them out of my life. I really figured he would never wake, that he would just be a shell that she had to force feed and whose ass she would have to wipe forever, and I thought she deserved exactly that."

"But he woke up, didn't he?" Manning asked in a near whisper.

Arondale nodded. "Yes, he did. And she took him home, and that's that. That is all I can tell you. Now arrest me."

Cohen cleared his throat. "Oh, we will, but there are a few more things we need to ask first. For instance, you have had no contact with Melvin since he left the hospital?"

"Not directly, no. His mother kept me posted, and from the sounds of it, he has been doing remarkably well."

Torrey asked, "Do you think, considering the brain injury he suffered, the abuse at his mother's hands, and the fact that you guys dug around in his brain with spoons might make him capable of... kidnapping girls... or worse?"

Now two tears ran down Arondale's face, and he buried his face in his hands in shame. After a few seconds, he looked up and looked at each of them briefly in the eye. His answer was all they needed to hear.

"I think, and this is my professional opinion, that between Adele Frink, myself, and Fitzsimmons and his team, we created a monster who, without a conscience, is capable of any violent act under the sun. More than likely he dreams about them."

CHAPTER 17

Melvin was still sitting in the corner, worshipping his sleeping mother, humming to music, and reminiscing about the great sex they had while the cops were talking to Arondale. He had been like that for hours, his other pets forgotten. He had already planned their disposal, and now he was planning the perfect future with Mother.

But Green Eyes wasn't sleeping; the last thing on her mind was getting her rest, as "Ken" put it. She had lain in the cell on her stinking mat, whispering between her cell and that of Princess. She was trying to wake up the girl to help her.

Finally, she gave up on her neighbor, and her legs got a bit stronger. She focused her hearing on Melvin, who seemed to be singing the songs to his sexually satiated, brain-dead mother.

It was time, there was no room for fear of death; she was going to die down here anyway. No, she needed to rush to battle with this madman like a warrior who had nothing to lose, because she didn't.

She fished out the syringe and gripped it in her right hand, then uncapped the long needle and tossed the cap on her mat. Green Eyes looked it over to make sure it was full of air, even pumping it a couple of times. Now she just had to worry about being quiet enough to sneak up on him and stick the thing in his jugular. She paused then, thinking that maybe the air shot to the brain was a better idea. No, if she had to face him, he would overcome her in a heartbeat. She had to sneak.

Slowly, and ever so carefully, Green Eyes began to open the heavy cell door. She pulled it inward a fraction of an inch... no creak. Another fraction... still no creak. The next time she pulled it a couple of inches, and it whined a bit. She froze up, her heart pounding, and listened for him to come, but all he did was keep singing.

When there was just enough of an opening in the door, Green Eyes slid out. She looked up and down the corridor in terror; what was this place? It was dank and dusty, with medical supplies strewn here and there. There appeared to be a big oven and a couple of other doors that were closed. Across the hall were more doors; Princess' cell, and it looked like it was shut and locked securely. It sounded to her like her captor was in the next cell down. She could see the door was partially open, as an arc of light was leaking out into the dank corridor. Outside of the room was a radio with music playing on it, and he was singing along word for word.

Green Eyes crept by Princess' cell and peeked in the small window, but Princess hadn't moved a muscle in hours. As a matter of fact, she looked pasty and gray, and her fingers were turning blue.

Green Eyes was sure the girl was dead. That meant she was on her own. If she didn't play this just right, she was going to be next, and she knew it.

"Goodbye, Princess," she mouthed silently; exhausted and tired of being afraid, she continued towards his mother's cell. Then when she looked to the right, she saw an opened door. Inside were boxes of what appeared to be supplies of all sorts. There was also a large knife sitting on a chair that was propping the door open; next to that was a bloody baseball bat. It was perfect; now she would have a fighting chance.

Green Eyes would take a step toward the mother's cell, then stop and listen. She would take another and do the same. It was only about six or seven steps from the open storage to his mother's, but it seemed to take her more than ten minutes to reach the cell.

There he was. He was crouched down with his knees to his chest, rocking back and forth and singing to his mom. She was beaten to a pulp, but she was only sleeping, a weird grin plastered to her face. Her hair was a tangled mess, and Green Eyes could smell sex and blood coming from the room.

Ken had his back to the door, and to her, and as far as she could tell, he didn't hear her at all. She took another step and hoped she could fit through the opening in the door without getting his attention, but she decided then and there that it didn't matter; he may kill her, but he was going to die getting the job done.

Green Eyes took a deep breath, and rushed through the doorway to Melvin Frink... entering the bloody doorway, with the bat in one hand and the knife in the other, she violently stabbed the man in the back too many times to count. When he finally fell to the floor, hardly able to hold up his arms to protect himself, she used the bat and beat him in the head until his skull was nearly split in two.

Afraid he was still alive, Denise made her way down the corridor, the naked, abused woman lay screaming behind her. It wasn't until she left his mother's cell that she registered the fact that the woman was screaming, over and over.

She ran out of the cellar, up the stairs, and found her way to the front door. The only thing on her mind was getting away because she was sure he was right behind her.

∞

Search warrant in hand, Lieutenant Cohen and Detective Miller of the Baltimore Police Department pulled up to the massive wrought iron gate that served as the doorway to the massive stone wall surrounding the Frink estate. Torrey and Manning were in the back seat, and they were followed by four other police cars and a single swat van full of men and women, ready to turn the place inside out.

Cohen was in the driver's seat of the lead vehicle, and he pulled up to the gate, stopping directly between the two huge stone columns on either side. The column on the left had an elaborate black box attached to it that measured about twelve by eighteen inches. Cohen rolled down his window and punched the "Call" button. It buzzed loudly until he released it, then he sat and waited for a response.

"I'm pretty sure if this is our man that no one is going to be answering the door, sir," Miller pointed out.

Cohen sighed and shook his head. "Procedure, Miller. How did you make detective, anyway?"

He punched the button once again, longer this time, almost to the point that it was annoying to all of them, making them squirm in their seats. Cohen pushed the "Call" button one final time, then hit "Speak."

"This is the Baltimore Police Department, Lieutenant Cohen speaking," he said. "I am here to see either Adele or Melvin Frink. Are either parties home at this time?"

He listened and got complete silence. He hit "Speak" again. "Hello, if anyone is inside, I need to make you aware that we have a warrant to search the premises at this address, including all buildings and vehicles outside of the home and the land itself from top to bottom. If you are home, it is best to cooperate; it will be much easier on everyone. If you are not, I must still announce that we have the legal right to enter the premises under any means necessary to serve this warrant through to completion."

Cohen then picked up his radio handset and said to the cars and SWAT team behind him, "Prepare to make forceful entry."

Torrey turned around and looked out the rear window to see SWAT members jumping from their truck, each one hitting the ground running and heading full-speed toward the gate. The other officers remained in their cars, alert and ready for whatever was to come next.

Two of the SWAT members attacked the gate with a blowtorch, and it didn't take long before they were able to swing open the two doors and hold them for the police vehicles to pass through. The other SWAT team members ran on foot ahead, leading the way up the long, snaking drive that led to the giant mansion.

Just as they were going around the first curve to the right, it happened.

A girl, bloodied and beaten nearly unrecognizable, was running up the drive toward them, screaming at the top of her lungs. She was naked, and her body was covered in cuts and bruises. Blood ran from between her legs, and her hair was so blood-soaked that the color couldn't be identified.

At first, she didn't seem to register that the police were right in front of her. She kept screaming; she continued to look over her shoulder as she ran as if she were expecting her pursuer to be right behind her, ready to pounce and beat her down to the ground. Her eyes were as wide as saucers and filled with sick terror.

Torrey didn't miss a beat. He jumped from the back seat of the cruiser and ran to the girl to stop her, but she nearly bowled him over, she ran with such force. His three cohorts were right behind him, with Miller on his phone calling for an ambulance. Torrey finally stopped her by bear hugging her and lifting her off the ground; she fought and fought with all she had, and all the while he said, over and over in a loud voice, "We're the police... we are here to help you. You're safe now!"

The police lit on the house like a swarm of flies on a pile of manure. Torrey stayed with the girl, who was half out of her mind with hysterics. He wanted to go in and help, to find out what was inside of that horrible place, but he realized that he was assigned a certain job, and caring for this young lady was his for now.

He wrapped her in his coat and held her to his chest, letting her sob and scream, her body jerking with trauma and shock.

"You're going to be fine now. It's all over. I've got you, honey. I've got you, and you're going to go home."

R.W.K. Clark

EPILOGUE

Six Months Later

The house in Guilford was almost gone.

As construction workers toiled away at leveling the house and all of the outbuildings completely, including the stone wall and gate, neighbors and gawkers from near and far, crowded around where the gate had once stood and watched as much as they could. It was safe to say that the city of Baltimore was glad to see the Frink house being demolished.

Denise Hoskins was one of those watching. Today, her long brown hair was clean, and she wore a touch of makeup, a modest blouse, and a pair of faded jeans with thongs on her feet. She had a smile of satisfaction on her face, but her stomach was sick. The place was hell, a torture chamber, and a prison. Not just for her, but for the man who had brought her there as well.

Tired of the demolition, Denise turned and began to walk to her car, which was parked half-a-block away. Just as she reached it, she looked up and saw John Torrey standing next to it. He was smiling, and he was wearing street clothes, which made him almost seem unrecognizable.

"Officer Torrey, hello! Look at you! Are you on vacation?" Denise greeted.

Torrey gave a hearty laugh. "Vacation? After this case, I threw in the towel and retired. I don't ever want to deal with a case like this again. How are you holding up?"

Denise shrugged. "Okay, I guess. Dreams keep coming, but I'm in therapy, and it's helping. It's not really something you ever forget, you know?"

"You're telling me. You know, Melvin Frink was so horribly victimized that he could only do the same to others, but what kills me is that it actually took a physical injury to bring it out of him. Strange how that works."

Denise looked over her shoulder at the house and thought about what he said. "I don't think the injury alone did it. I think he would have been fine, abuse and all if they just hadn't fiddled with his mind. You know, people are terribly traumatized every day, but they don't run out and do the things that this monster did. I blame him, sure, but most of all, I blame all the rest of them, the ones who thought he was nothing more than a thing to be experimented on and used. Like his mother."

"Well, she won't see the light of day for a long time, if ever. Adele Frink is locked up at Northern State's Psych Hospital, and she is in the maximum diagnosis ward. I've been told she's so violent and sick they have to keep her in restraints constantly."

Denise smiled. "Good, It's where she belongs. Well, I'd better go. I'm hitting the road, Torrey. Time to get out of Baltimore and see the world." She unlocked her car door and climbed inside, then started the ignition. Rolling down the window, she said to him, "Thank you for just holding me that day. That was all I needed... I just needed to be safe, and you kept me safe."

"Anytime kid. You, be safe."

With a smile, Denise Hoskins pulled away from the curb and drove away a different person. She was stronger and had her feet on the ground now, and thanks to Melvin Frink, she had the tools to help others feel safe the way Torrey had done for her.

As her small red car faded into the distance, Torrey watched her smiling. Monsters were real, that was for sure. But if he'd learned anything, it was that warriors and victors were too, and the strongest one he had ever met just drove away from the nightmare forever...

ENTREATY

This book was made possible by reviews from readers like you. Reviews fuel my creativity. If you enjoyed this novel, I implore you to please write a review and share your experience on the retailer's website. The livelihood for authors is entirely dependent on reviews, and I must say, it is the largest obstacle as a struggling author that I have encountered. Please tell a friend, tell a loved one about this read. With your help, I will be one step closer to overcoming this obstacle. In return, I thank you from the bottom of my heart, and sincerely appreciate your time and effort.

Humbled, with gratitude,

R.W.K. Clark

ABOUT THE AUTHOR

I am a father of two beautiful children, Jon and Kim. They are my motivating forces; they are the lighthouse in this vast ocean. In my life, they are the air that I breathe; they are the oasis in this desert of uncertainty. They are my greatest joy in life and my number one priority. I have a long list of hobbies, and I attribute that to my lust for life! I like to surround myself with positive people, who share the same interests. Family values, the arts, outdoors, nature, and travel are tops on my list. I embrace attending cultural and artistic events because I believe dramatic self-expression is the window to the soul. I wear my heart on my sleeve, and I still believe in chivalry, and I always treat people the way I want to be treated.

www.rwkclark.com